Both Sides of My Skin

Both Sides of My Skin

By

Elizabeth Trach

AnnorlundaBooks

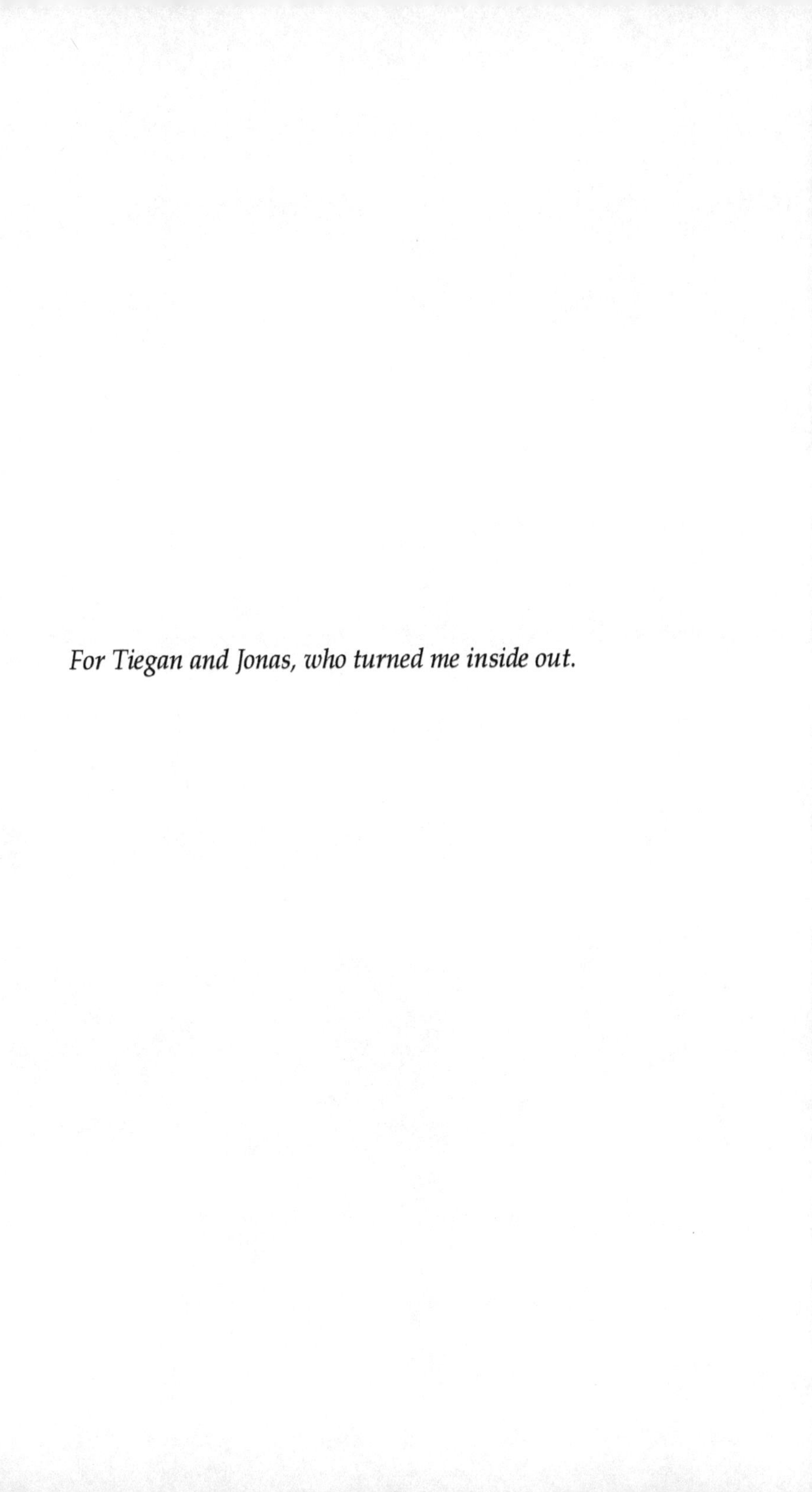

For Tiegan and Jonas, who turned me inside out.

Contents

Recognition

"The day I brought you home from the hospital," my mother says, crossing one leg over the other and letting it bob lightly in the air, "was cold. There were flurries, and that was May seventeenth. All I had on was this loose yellow sundress with straps because I wanted something pretty for your first day at home." She hunches her shoulders to click up a light for her cigarette, then waves the smoke away from me. "Will the smoke bother the baby?"

"No, Mom, it's fine." The baby, still tucked away under layers of skin and fat and fluid, is safe for now, although I don't know how to tell my mother that she won't be able to visit her granddaughter if she's going to smoke. She probably won't need to as long as her visits are in the afternoon. When I was about six or seven, I remember hearing her side of a phone conversation with my grandmother, and feeling funny to hear her call someone "Mom." They talked about ulcers, which I thought sounded like a bad stomachache. Later she explained that they came from worrying about things. I didn't understand why she would be afraid of getting ulcers when all she did was play with me and my sister during the day while my father was at work, but soon after that she gave up coffee and switched to tea with a cigarette first thing in the morning. As far as I know, her digestive system is fine, but gathering up her energy to face the day is a ritual she still observes, even though my sister and I have long since moved out of the house and don't require any special vigor from her anymore.

She leans back into the metal café chair and holds the cigarette as far away from me as she can, careful to let the wisps of smoke rise into the air beyond the umbrella over our table so it won't somehow be trapped in my breathing space. She exhales. "Well, anyway, your father forgot to bring me a coat, but I don't remember being cold at all. I just remember holding you tight in your hospital blanket, watching your face watching the snow somewhere over my shoulder. You didn't blink the whole ride home."

It's hard to imagine my parents as young as Rick and I are now, wrapped in joy and expectation. I've seen pictures, but the gold and browns of the furniture and clothes, the wide ties and polyester sheen on everything, the glasses that darkened in the burnt-smelling glare of the flash cube all take away from their faces, make them seem like strangers.

The effeminate young waiter delivers our lunch with a flourish and a smile. He's awfully cheerful for Sunday brunch, working for a tip, and I will slip him some extra to make up for the embarrassing twelve percent my mother will add to the bill she insists on paying. This morning all I could think about was eggs, but now that an enormous ham and cheese omelet is in front of me, I know I'll only be able to pick at it. There's not much room left for my stomach inside me, so even though I am hungry all the time I can't eat much anymore.

"So, do you think that you're ready for the delivery? I mean, is the baby's room ready? And you packed a little overnight bag for yourself?"

"Yes and yes. I think we're all set. Birthing class is done, so I practice the relaxation and meditation techniques every night now, and Rick guides me through this glove-relaxation thing where I practice touching parts of my body to numb them."

"Does that work? I mean, I don't really know … the C-section was so easy with you that I just signed right up for another one for your sister."

I take my time chewing. The way I was born is the exact opposite of how I plan to have my baby. No interventions, no drugs, no men in white coats telling me what to do without me asking some serious questions first. This is mine. Mine and Rick's, not some guy's lunch break between rounds of golf. My mother has no idea what giving birth felt like, so it's hard for us to talk about. She can't tell me what I want to know.

"But I know, you want to do it natural. I think it's good to try, to go as far as you can. But if you are in pain, you should let them give you something. It's all so different now, you know, how they even let you have people in the room …"

So this is what it's really about, why she got up early on a Sunday, when I know she fell asleep in her reclining chair the night before while watching tapes of the week's talk shows. I try to navigate this lightly but quickly, like hurrying over a patch of ice: the less contact, the better.

"Yeah, well, it will just be Rick and me. Kind of private and calm, something we need to do together." I press on past the circled day on the calendar in my mind. "We want some time to be together as a family for a while, the three of us, before any visitors. Probably a week or two."

"Oh. Oh, I figured that. I think you had said that. But if you feel like you need help—not with the baby or anything, but with cooking or cleaning up, then I can come and stay for a few days. Whenever you decide."

I don't remind my mother that Rick does all the cooking, and that we split the cleaning. I have trouble picturing her doing these things that she hasn't done for years. Rick says I have her trained to be the ideal laissez-faire mom, but I remember when, in a burst of frustration with a wad of tulle, I asked her for help making my wedding veil. She was ready with an idea right then, and I realized that she had been watching, either waiting or wishing for me to need her. She smiled a lot that night, and it ended up being fun, but when she told me how glad she was that we got to do this together, the sharing ideas and the solving problems and the mindless chatter about flowers and food, I felt like a teenager who doesn't let her little sister watch her get ready for a date.

Suddenly the air in my lungs is pressed out of me, from within. I shift and stretch in my seat, trying to somehow make myself taller so the baby's feet aren't jammed so far into my airspace. I imagine the baby curling her toes to get a foothold between my ribs and using the muscles in between them as a springboard, trying to get leverage to push her head toward the light. Not yet, I think.

"Not so much room left after eight months, huh?" My mother puts down her fork and slides her chair around the small table. She reaches a hand toward my belly. "Is she kicking?"

When was the last time my mother touched my stomach? When she tickled me as a toddler? When I was nine and made myself sick over a detention for leaving my viola in the coat rack? Or was it involuntary, a lightning stab across the car as she jammed on the brakes, even though I was already old enough to drive myself wherever we were going?

My mother's hand on my stomach doesn't feel any different than the hands of all the other people, strangers or friends, who have reached out to touch me since I started to show back in the spring. I'm not quite used to this, my body being available for anyone who needs contact: patted from the outside, kicked from the inside.

"Oh, now that she knows I want her to move, she's not going to. That reminds me of you." She takes her hand back to rest on her own stomach, the soft mound of menopausal fat an echo of what she is feeling for in her memory. "But enjoy it now, because soon you won't be able to keep her from moving. Even though you love her more than anything else."

"Her and Rick, you mean."

"No, just her. The way I love both you and your sister more than I love your father." I feel a squirmy flutter at the point of my breastbone, and it's not the baby this time. I have never been comfortable with the things my mother was so willing to share after my father divorced her. There are things that I know about them, about my mother and all her feelings, that I don't want to know. Things that I pretend I don't know, even though she seems to want to tell me, the way you suddenly gush everything out at a slumber party to girls who, in their pajamas in the dark, seem just like you, and you hope that it doesn't come back as something ugly and misunderstood in the fluorescence of a junior high hallway.

"Yeah, but you and dad aren't married anymore. Rick and I ... are."

"It doesn't matter. This is something I realized long before. Your father forgot my coat, but I didn't need it. Dogwood petals were curling up under the snow and dropping, but I didn't feel the cold. I felt you."

I think about telling Rick what my mother said, but when he looks up from pulling suckers off the almost-ripe tomato plants and asks, "How was brunch?", all I say is "Fine, but I'm tired now," and in the house I close doors and pull shades for a dark, cool nap. A day passes and another, and I know I won't tell him, that it would seem stranger to him than it does to me, that he would want to laugh away our failure to understand. There are many things I don't tell him now, because I will not be able to explain what it's like to have my body controlled by someone else, to feel a stranger inside yet not to feel her, the way we only feel our stomachs when they make demands. The baby is and isn't, just like I am and am not myself anymore. But I think about the way my mother splits herself open for me, spills out whatever's inside, sometimes sweet like watermelon, sometimes hot and sticky like blood. She flows; I'd rather avoid a mess.

Days are warm now, midsummer, so I take my walks in the morning. I need the exercise to get stronger, to keep up my stamina for the birth, but when I get to the playground down the street, I stop to sit on the bench by the sandbox. I know that there will be no rest periods in labor, but I stop anyway. I'm not ready for the real thing; I need more time to practice relaxing and preparing myself to feel the pain as something other than pain. More time to massage and stretch myself out ahead of time so I don't tear apart.

My feet feel better without all the extra weight on them, and the air is still morning-cool. A little boy with hair cut too short to curl plays alone in the sandbox, building whole cities and digging tunnels to connect them, creating countries and empires. Every now and then he smashes them and rebuilds, so intent on his work that he doesn't know I am watching him. He is sturdy, confident; his command of the sandbox scares me a bit in its utter independence.

I am startled by the wet grind of an old man clearing his throat as he thuds down on the bench next to me. I blink to focus on him, so much closer to me than the boy, and I wonder how long I have been staring off into space. This isn't the first time I have been surprised to find that the world has shifted around me while I was busy being pregnant. So much of my time is spent just sitting, and for the first time I can remember, spent not thinking. Or else thinking so far on the inside that it's not in words or even pictures, but somewhere my body takes me. But it's not nothing, because when I get snapped back I can feel that things on the inside have shifted too, have pressed forward just a sliver of a degree in their trajectory. The groaning push of earth; tectonic plates in their slow, inevitable passage.

The man looks at me and nods. Large-knuckled hands on the hard ridge of his thighs, he eases back against the bench, letting it prop him up. He looks as though he has never had to shave, skin translucent with age, still more peachy than sallow. It is still firm over his cheeks, and he probably doesn't look old when he smiles, but farther down his face the skin has been pulled into sagging flaps around the jaw and neck. His eyes are blue.

In silence except for the sparrows and the traffic, we watch the boy continue his construction. I feel the muffled tapping from inside my belly, its taut dome like a large, smooth egg. I look down and can see a small section of my big turquoise shirt rippling up and down: the baby's hand, maybe foot, pushing against its boundaries. I am ready to shift position, maybe to move on, when a screech from the sandbox slices the air.

"No no NO! I don't WANT to! I want to stay here!" The boy smashes his shovel into the dirt and turns to look up at his mother, who has come up behind him. She holds out her hand to him across the low wall of the sandbox.

"Honey, it's time to go home and have lunch. You want to eat a good sandwich, don't you? You must be hungry with all this playing." The woman says this sweetly, more calmly than I could have managed, and more nicely than he deserves. She places her palm on his head.

"NO!" The boy, face twisted in rage that is not softened by the curves of his baby fat, flicks his shovel up, flinging sand into his mother's eyes. She steps back, off-balance, and brushes at her eyes with her hand.

The old man sighs, and I turn to him in time to see him give a slow, tight-lipped shake of his head. In profile he looks like my grandmother: paper-dry skin at the throat, and gray-white hair, too long for a man but too short on my grandmother, wisping around the collar. The firm, round cheek forming a shelf under the sunken eye.

What I remember most clearly about visits with my grandmother is her Lazy Susan on the Formica kitchen table. She lived in a farmhouse that smelled like cats and seemed to be falling down around her, floors listing and creaking under her weight. She would stand in the kitchen, round-backed and arthritic, pouring tea while my mother admonished us not to spin the Lazy Susan. My sister and I loved it, loved to watch the honey bear, sugar, salt, pepper, torn envelopes scribbled with phone numbers, the little calendar from the IGA with a flag for each federal holiday, and the amber prescription bottles all whirl past again and again, turning and returning to us in a blurry version of themselves.

"What's the difference, Miriam? A little spinning isn't hurting anything," my grandmother always said. "They'll be spinning off for real soon enough."

"That's not the point, Mom," my mother's voice was brittle. "This is my thing to deal with, not yours." She huffed out a pouty, exasperated sigh. The Lazy Susan ground to a halt, and I looked over it at my little sister, who had shrunk down into her chair, eyes wide. I sat up; I couldn't decide if my mother sounded like a grown-up or a kid, or if she thought my grandmother was one of us for a minute.

My grandmother, unruffled, sat and sipped her tea. "Yes, but I know how it will turn out. Just enjoy them while you still have them." My grandmother gave the Lazy Susan a spin.

The scrape of my mother's chair as she pushed away from the table vibrated through the floor and into my chest, with an almost musical overtone in the metal chair legs. Her tea sloshed over the edge of the chipped cup and ran down into the saucer. She opened the back window and lit a cigarette. "I'm not you," she breathed out, sound and smoke floating out the window toward the doghouse of her long-dead childhood pet.

"Mm hmm. All you can do with kids,"—a broken cough—"is love the shit out of them." I blink, and the old man is looking at me. The sky is white and hazy, but bright, and I'm not sure if the androgynous, age-cracked voice is in my memory or if it is real. I feel a centrifugal pull at the pit of my stomach, as if suddenly the earth has stopped spinning and I have been thrown, waiting for things to fall back into place around me. All kinds of people give all kinds of advice when you're pregnant, and a stranger's good intentions are nothing unusual, but his bushy eyebrows are raised as though he expects a reply.

"The thing is, they will never love you back as much as you love them." I'm not sure what he's talking about and feel choked by confusion, embarrassment. He looks straight ahead to the empty sandbox, eyes following the mother and son as they turn onto the sidewalk for home. "Maybe, if you're lucky and if you live long enough, you see it in how they love their own kids, and that'll do." His voice is soft; he could be talking to himself. He shifts his weight again to look first at my belly and then at my face. "My wife never believed me when I tried to tell her this."

I try to smile, but mostly I just want to get home. My stomach has been bothering me off and on today, and I feel now like I really, really need to use the bathroom. I feel nervous and full. I pull myself up, and except for my feet, it feels good to stand and have the baby's weight on other parts of me. "Enjoy the weather," I say, and it sounds stupid and small out there on the air. I walk, and the baby is a lumbering pendulum in the space where my legs hinge to my body.

When I get home Rick is in the garden, weeding. He waves, and I continue straight into the house. The bathroom is cool and dark, and I sit. Rick is home? It must be Saturday. For me the days are all the same: breathing, eating, sleeping, walking. The weekends are a little different because Rick is added to the background while I do these things, or while they are done to me, which is how it feels sometimes. I push against the pressure I feel, the hard lump of gas, but nothing happens. Again, and again, but the room feels small and I want to be outside with lots of space and air on my skin.

In the garden the tomatoes are still green, with just a hint of blushing at their tops. I used to think that tomatoes turned red slowly, a progression from green to yellow to orangey-pink and then, finally, red. Since we dug out these garden plots, though, I have never seen a season when this is true. Really, one day they are green, and the next they are red. I don't know if the change is too fast to see, or it's just that I grew forgetful and stopped looking for it, but I have never been able to follow one tomato's ripening step by step.

Rick comes and sits down next to me under the cherry tree. He sits until his breathing slows from pants to regular pace; he has been working hard getting the garden to grow this year without my help. "Julia, are you feeling alright?" he asks me.

I am sitting cross-legged, rocking back and forth a little. I don't want to stop, but I do, to show him I can. But stillness doesn't feel right, so I start up again, forward and back. The sky has become white-damp, and my fingers are glistening fat like sausage links, swelled numb with water they seem to pull out of the air when the weather turns humid. "I'm fine. It just feels like there's a lot of pressure today. I keep feeling like I have to go to the bathroom, but then I don't. I don't know. I was practicing the glove-relaxation thing, so when it bothers me I put my hand on my stomach until I feel better."

He smiles. "As long as it's just a stomachache, I guess that's good. If this were three weeks from now, I'd be wondering if you were in labor. You're making some pretty interesting faces every now and then." He rubs my back, and it feels foreign. "Wanna drink?"

With Rick off in the house I feel better. I need space; I don't want to be touched. Or watched. I want to move around, to pace the garden up and back, or at least just to rock. In labor? It's still three weeks away, and I need to practice so much more before then. I'm not ready. Not ready for the pain, or to let this baby push its way into my life. I thought before that I might not be ready to let the baby sleep between us in our bed at night, but at least that part now seems okay. Rick doesn't know this, but I haven't wanted him to touch me for a while. There's so much going on during the day on the inside of me, so much touching and fluttering and kicking, that at night I just can't take any more. I try to brace myself for the patting of a hand or the good night kiss so I don't pull away when he reaches for me across the too-soft tangle of sheets. He wouldn't understand, and it would hurt him, even though it doesn't mean anything. It's hard to tell what anything means this summer, or what we, the three of us, will look like in the clear, cool light of fall.

The baby gives a good, sharp kick, straight up, and my whole body clenches. I stoop over, and while I wait to unfurl again, I am aswim in one of my earliest memories, one that is all flash and scent. I remember sitting in the front part of a shiny silver grocery cart, and all the wet green smells of the produce section. I was swinging my legs at the knees, idly, liking the feel of them dangling and moving in time. My toes bumped, bumped, bumped lightly into my mother's stomach as she pushed the cart. "No. Stop that," she hissed in my ear. I looked in her eyes, narrowed under dark brows. I pulled back my legs and kicked her as hard as I could. She gasped, and looked at me, in shock, then down at some peaches. I knew I had won something, a kernel of power over my mother that I could bury in cool darkness and wait for, even though I didn't know quite what food I would reap from it to store against future famine.

Rick follows my pacing along the tomato rows to hand me a glass of ice water. When we first met, his eyes would have strayed to my breasts, compact and upturned, "expectant," he murmured once, tickling my ear with his breath. Even just a few months ago he would have been looking into my eyes, studying my forehead to determine what mood the lines there revealed. Now, surrounded by all the growing things that are ours, his eyes rest on my stomach, the largest part of me, the one thing that grows without him pruning and prodding it into being. He watches me pace, my belly brushing the tangy, summer-scented leaves of the tomato plants that haven't been tied to their stakes yet. "Are you ever going to stop?"

"Not yet. I'm thinking." This isn't exactly true, at least not as far as I can tell on the surface of things, but again, something is crawling forward in me while the plants grow and Rick pours water and my feet tread the grass down along the garden path.

The ringing of the phone slices the air and jars me awake. I haven't been sleeping, exactly, but sort of floating in semiconsciousness on the sofa, practicing laying my hands on my stomach when it starts to hurt again. These pains come and go, and I press my hand low on the underside of the baby until I can relax away the gassy pains I've had all day.

"Julia, phone's for you. It's your mom." I prop myself up, sweaty, and start to shake my head, but Rick is half-turned to the wall and can't, or won't, see me. "Yeah, we're heading into the home stretch now. Hold on, Miriam, here she comes. Yes. Actually, I think she's feeling a little under the weather today—"

I swipe the phone out of Rick's hand. "Hey, Mom." I glare at Rick, but he shrugs and smiles, sits in my spot on the couch and starts to flip through the channels. "How are you?"

"Hey Julia, I know you're busy, but the reason I was calling is to see if you wanted some of the baby stuff I came across this weekend. I was going through your old clothes and toys and found Duckie and Blue Blankie. I just thought maybe you'd want them back now."

I don't really remember these toys. Their names sound familiar, but only as words I have heard in family stories, not out of a genuine memory of the things themselves. "Um, okay, but what kind of shape are they in? Good for a baby?"

"Well, to tell you the truth, I haven't washed them yet. I'm a little afraid they might fall apart if we try to clean them up." She pauses, and in the background I can hear the faint, canned applause from her television. Her talk shows: the self-help week in review. "I wouldn't want to hurt them, so why don't I just bring them over and you can decide what you want to do with them. You know, whenever you're ready after the baby is born ..." I feel my stomach clenching up again, and I breathe out around it, willing myself to relax against it, to do the opposite of what my body wants to do and un-stiffen. "… Do you think you have any idea of when that might be?"

I haven't been listening, and her voice is falsely bright, irritating. I can't listen to people talk and concentrate on breathing or touching away the pain at the same time. Rick has done the same thing throughout the day, too; he keeps chattering, offering drinks and snacks and pillows for my feet. Or worse, he reaches for me with hands that still have dirt under the nails and ground into the grooves of his fingerprints. I need quiet to remind myself to squash down the pricks of fear that creep up into the back of my throat: I am not in labor. It is not yet time to let go.

"No. I mean, I haven't thought about it yet. Like I said before, we'll probably want a couple weeks as a family. There's no rush on bringing old stuff over; we've got lots of shower gifts, so I don't think we *need* anything."

My mother sniffs. "Oh, I know. And I know Rick is great at helping out around the house." I cringe at this: What my mother sees as Rick's benevolence is what I see simply as his fair share, and this is the thing she will never understand about our marriage. This discussion always makes me feel like I'm getting away with something. "But you'll both be tired, and I just thought I could help …" More applause, then silence. I imagine the click of her lighter, think of her holding the cigarette as far away from the mouthpiece of the phone as she can. I will not pick up this thread, and the silence stretches tight into faintly desperate static. Another burst of applause is cut off abruptly, and she says "But that's okay. It's not like I have anything planned for the next couple months, so I'll be here if you decide to call. Just let me know if you ever need me."

I can't tell whether or not this was calculated to make me feel like one of those newly-popular high school girls who suddenly realizes how awkward her best friend from middle school is, and has one last, good day before ignoring her the rest of the school year. I feel that pang of guilt, but also the frustration, the indignant counter that if she just *tried* a little harder, maybe learned to hide her feelings a bit and put on some makeup, acted cooler, she could fit in with the older kids, too.

Why doesn't she try? When I picture myself with the baby, I can fast-forward through her childhood and see her as an adult woman: beautiful, kind, intelligent, of course; but also independent, a companion who no longer needs me to give something, but rather chooses me, wants me. This faceless daughter recognizes the part of me that I have saved for myself, and likes it that way, enjoys having a mother who is a person. We are not slick with tears and sweat and the wetness of things we can't keep contained, so I don't need to try so hard to hold onto something so slippery as my mother has made me.

My feet have made a little puddle of sweat on the floor. They are not hot, but so swollen that the arches have flattened out against the floor and there is no space between my toes. The wave of tightness in my stomach is gone, and I feel lighter. "So Mom, what other toys did you find?" Maybe I will remember one, or maybe hearing about the way I was when I was little will help me feel that my mother is somehow bigger.

Another dark wave crescendos toward me, pushing in on my vision from the edges until I'm no longer seeing but only feeling as I lean forward to press into it, doing what it wants me to do. They call it pushing, call out numbers across the antiseptic room, but I have lost count and follow it through the haze until it recedes and my spine uncurls and I can see the outline of my husband and feel his hand on mine. Other people have their palms on me but I don't feel them, only the stretching or the not stretching around the patch of hair that widens and shrinks in the tide of my flesh.

In the rosy glow there is a clock, white sheets, gloved hands. The crest of my stomach flanked by my knees: still-lifes of something done through me, not by me. Warm whispers in my ear, metallic tinkling at my feet. Graying light, muscles clench to attention. Again.

All afternoon when Rick asked I told him, "No, don't be silly, it's still three weeks away." All through the pressure as it turned to a downward squeezing across my abdomen, until I could no longer talk when it was happening. Rick made me come to the hospital then, in the dusk that was humid and weighted, even though I told him the nurses would laugh and send us home again. I was sure I wasn't in labor. It wasn't time yet.

It isn't time. It's three weeks too soon, and the baby and I both are small and weak. I am not ready to push her out, to live through the blinding tremors that shake out from the center of me, vibrating me apart from the inside out. I want to keep her inside me, to hold her back. To keep her and me and even Rick from what's coming. I don't know what it is, but it doesn't stop pushing through me to get to her. I'm not doing anything except trying to hold us together.

But nothing I think or do can keep my body from pushing her out. Muscles clench and crush so hard that it pulls me forward, sitting, and I push without wanting to, without thinking or listening to the counts the nurses call out so crisply. What else will come out of me unbidden? Is there anything left to keep inside, or will it all come roaring out and leave my husk behind on the birthing bed? Even these thoughts last only as long as the lull between contractions, and then are pressed out of me by the force of my labor again and again.

The yawning tightness at my core is the same each time, and if I am tired I don't feel it as I am carried along by a force so insistent that it can't be mine. Leaning forward into the blackness, a wet pop and slippery, fast slide as the taut skin suddenly deflates. And I know. "There's her head!" someone says, and I am surprised at the way I imagine she must be, dangling halfway between me and the world, not yet a real baby but not totally swallowed up and protected inside me, either. I can't tuck her back in. And for the first time, I don't want to anymore: I need more than anything to get her out of me, to make her a person and not something attached to me. I let go of Rick's hand.

They say to wait but I won't, and for the first time I seize the oncoming surge and feel in charge of my body. Another crunch, some lumpy parts sliding through, and I fall into the starchy pillow behind. I close my eyes and hear her unmuffled cry, her first pain soaring out above my hours-old one. I am quiet while she pitifully wails: I've already spilled out everything I have with the unnoticed afterbirth, and will spend a lifetime unable to pull it back inside. I glimpse the thick, round sac of it, though, before the nurse tosses it into a stainless steel pan, and it is surprisingly blue, lined with veins as prominent the ones in a bodybuilder's biceps. It is smaller than the baby; she has grown strong from its richness, and there will never be anything I can give her that will answer her needs as perfectly as the placenta that once curved around her ossifying bones.

She is on my stomach now, but I can't feel her because we are still the same. Both warm: my sweat, her amniotic brine. Her eyes are dark and wide, brow wrinkled in concentration on my face. This is the creature who was kicking me so insistently on the inside, and I know looking in her shriveled, old-man face that she will kick me again here on the outside. I don't know what she sees when she looks at me, but think maybe the slickness of it all isn't messy to her yet, but comfortable. Looking each other in the face, recognition; and neither of us notices the cold gleam of the surgical scissors as they advance to cut the cord.

I have been stitched back together and wiped clean and left alone to wait for Rick to return from the baby's check-up in the nursery. My legs are heavy; they feel a part of the scratchy sheets that are wilting beneath my weight. The sheets are damp with sweat, and when I pull up the blanket I shiver until the cool spot I have shifted into warms to the temperature of my skin. I don't want to move, but somewhere in my chest I am too alert to sleep, and I am tired of waiting for Rick to come back so I have someone to talk to.

With a click the door opens and Rick shuffles heavily into the room. He rakes a hand up his forehead and through his hair, leaving it sticking up and ragged. "Hey," he breathes out, almost in a sigh, "How're you?"

I open my mouth to answer and don't know where to begin. I want to tell the whole story to him, how it felt from the first pains early in the day, before I even knew they were contractions, to all the activity at the hospital and up through the things he missed while he was gone. I want him to fill in the parts I can't remember, to help me understand all the things that have happened here. He can tell me the things I said, and what it all looked like from the outside. We can talk until I am finally sleepy, telling the story together.

Rick yawns, gaping and loud as a lion after a meal. His voice is low and raspy. "I'm actually not feeling so good. Achy, tired … I think I'm getting sick. I'm just exhausted." He presses my hand, and his palm is dry and hot against my cool, clammy one. His eyes look puffy, squinting, even in the dim room. "I really need some sleep so I can function tomorrow. I think I'm gonna go."

I nod and force out a cheerful "Okay."

"I'm so sorry. I feel really bad about leaving you alone … so I called your mom. She's coming to stay with you tonight." He leans a little closer and squeezes my hand. "She was really excited to come to the hospital. She's getting her bracelet at the nurse's station, and will be in with the baby in a little bit." He looks at me hopefully, then turns to cough into his fist.

"Fine." I shake off his hand and turn away from him to lie on my side. "At least give me a chance to pretend I'm asleep before she gets here." The energy in my chest spreads up my shoulders and tightens my jaw. This is not how I wanted this to be. These first hours were supposed to be for the two of us, the three of us, together. Now Rick is sick and weak, and I have no sympathy for him. He can't see my face, and I try to keep the anger out of my voice. "Go get some rest."

He pats my shoulder and sighs again. "Thanks. You get some rest too, and I'll be back in the morning. I love you."

"Mm hmm." I shift in the cold sheets to find a comfortable position. I close my eyes. I am not tired, but I do not have the energy to answer all my mother's questions when she gets here, or to brace myself against her stream of chatter. If she thinks I am asleep, maybe she'll turn on the TV, and we can both drift off to the murmur of some late-night infomercial that pretends to be a talk show.

My mother comes in loudly, bumping the stainless steel baby cart into the door and the foot of my bed. I pretend to stir, but keep my eyes closed. "Oh no, no, no. Let your mommy sleep. I'll tell you all about your mommy and what she was like when she was as little as you and I was the mommy. Your mommy kicked and squirmed and didn't like to stay in her blankets, and the nurses didn't know what to do with her ..."

When I finally dare to open my eyes to see my mother, she is sitting in the red vinyl chair next to my bed, cradling her granddaughter in her arms. Her head is bent to the baby's, murmuring her story. She looks conspiratorial; they could be sharing secrets in the predawn hush of the hospital room. I can't decide if she looks young or old: it is impossible to know how other people see her.

The bundle shifts and I hear a low, muffled cry. It is probably time to try nursing her again, even though I don't yet have any milk to give her. My mother reaches into her pocket and slips a bright pink pacifier into the blankets where the baby's mouth must be. "Your mommy liked these a lot, so much that when she was three I had to start hiding them one by one until they were all gone ..."

When we checked into the hospital, Rick and I filled out a questionnaire for the nursery, and specifically circled "no" in the section about pacifiers and formula. All the advice about breastfeeding goes against using pacifiers, yet here it is, and I am now, finally, too tired to argue about it. Who knows how long it will take to undo what my mother has done. Or maybe I won't want to: the baby is comforted, if only for the moment. But that might be enough.

I close my eyes and listen to my mother's words flow out of her, whispery murmurs that wash over me like water. She is doing all the talking that I had wanted to do with Rick, overflowing with the effort of putting all the feelings she's ever had into words for a baby who can't understand any of it. Tomorrow this is what I will try to do, too, and what the baby overhears in her clear plastic bassinet will be all rhythm and cadence without sense. My prattle will wake her, hungry and screaming for more milk than I have to give, and she will be frustrated by my delayed and imperfect response to her need. For now, though, she is quiet, and so am I. My mother speaks softly, ceaselessly, and I am cradled to sleep on a tide of words that I am only beginning to understand.

The Second Time

The first time wasn't like this. But this time, I knew right away, even before I was late, and long before the blood test confirmed it. Two days before I was due for my period, I was up late watching *ER* and was suddenly, uncontrollably crying when a mother lit herself on fire in front of her young son in the ambulance bay.

"That doesn't mean anything. It was just sad and you were tired staying up so late," my husband said.

But I knew. I never cry.

So I thought that the second time I would feel everything more, earlier, and with the expertise of an experienced mom who knows what is going on in her body. But the crying jag was the only thing I felt. The early weeks passed and there were no sore breasts, no waves of nausea at the smell of fish in the lunchroom, no bloated, crampy feeling in my pelvis.

"Michael, do my boobs look bigger to you?" I fling back the shower curtain and step out of the tub. Shaving at the sink, he looks tan against the gleaming white tile all around. He hands me a towel with his free hand.

"No, not really."

"You're not even looking. I feel like last time they were a lot bigger by now. And they don't hurt." I move the towel down from my head and start scrubbing over my shoulders, arms, and still flattish stomach.

"Emmie, there's a big range of normal. You're already all stretched out from before, so it doesn't bother you. Stop worrying so much."

"But it's just that I don't feel anything." He swishes the razor around in the scummy water. "Everyone I know at work who had a miscarriage said they didn't feel pregnant..."

"That's just anecdotal evidence. Feelings aren't necessarily reliable. Go look it up in my old OB-GYN text if you're that nervous about it."

With a sucking and muffled pop the water starts down the drain. Michael straightens his tie and turns to go. "I have a double tonight, so I won't be home until tomorrow morning. Kiss Sophie for me."

"Bye, Doc." I'd have kissed him good-bye, but he was already gone.

"Mamama. MamaMA." Sophie's insistence forces me to open my eyes. I have been lying on the couch trying to doze, but really I was just thinking and trying to feel something in my belly to reassure myself. I guess I could feel good about being so tired, but who isn't tired with an eighteen-month-old to chase after?

Sophie is standing in front of the television trying to push her *Baby Mozart* video back into the VCR. Maybe I dozed after all; it must have ended a few minutes ago, because the static is on now.

"MamaMAAAA."

"Okay, Soph." I hoist myself up off the crumpled beige cushions and turn off the TV. "How 'bout a story?"

She toddles over to the basket of books by the fireplace and pulls out *The Very Hungry Caterpillar*. "Mamama." She holds it out to me and smiles.

I pull her onto my lap on the couch and she scrunches down, rubbing her cheek on my stomach. It makes her stick-straight, baby-fine hair stand up with static. She's getting tired, too.

"Baba. Baba." She looks at me and says it again: "Baba." Then she stretches her arms as far as they will go around my waist and plants her face where my bellybutton would be if she could see it. "Baba."

"Baby?" I ask her, slow and singsong. "The baby lives there in Mommy's belly?" We'd been talking a lot about how babies live in their mommies' tummies, and how big sisters are loving and gentle with little babies. She never had shown much interest before, other than lifting her Dolly up for a kiss.

Sophie looks me straight in the eye for a moment. Somehow her eyes stayed blue, even though Michael's and mine are hazel. For a second she looks much older, like she really does know. She smiles and bobs her head up and down. "Baba!" Again she snuggles into my stomach and pries open the board book.

I think of calling Michael, but he wouldn't think this is news enough to have him paged.

There's a lump in my throat and the writing on the first page is blurry. "Thanks, Soph," I whisper and kiss her soft brown hair. I clear my throat. "In the light of the moon a little egg lay on a leaf."

Over a steaming bowl of mashed potatoes Michael asks, "How are you feeling today? You seem to be better the last few weeks. Not so uptight." He pours some gravy over his potatoes and chicken and looks up at me. "And not so tired."

"Well, it helps that I'm starting to show. And at sixteen weeks, my energy is back. There shouldn't be much to worry about anymore." I watch Sophie drop another piece of chicken neatly into her mouth. "And really, that night with Sophie made me just *know*."

Michael gives a close-mouthed cough and swallows. "Well, I'm glad you feel better, anyway." He doesn't believe me about Sophie. Just an emotional reaction to the release of hormones, he said. At least he hasn't rolled his eyes.

I swallow another gravy-ful scoop of potatoes and the phone rings. Michael pushes back his chair and it scrapes across the oak floorboards. "One night away from the hospital and the phone rings while we're eating," he mutters, shaking his head.

I spoon a bite of mashed potatoes into Sophie's open mouth. Really, she's too big to be spoon-fed, but she won't do mushy things herself—too messy. Sophie is a very meticulous eater: no cute pictures of a spaghetti-sauce-faced tot in her baby book. Each piece of fruit or chicken is picked up from the high chair tray in a perfect pincer grasp and grabbed neatly by her four front teeth. I practically never have to wipe her face, and the dog is eternally disappointed in his vigil at her feet.

"Emmie, it's for you. It's Naomi." He stands with the phone on his chest, brow creased in the middle.

My stomach flips at a rush of adrenaline, and for the first time in this pregnancy I feel like I'm going to throw up. Naomi is the nurse midwife; there's no reason for her to call this late except with the result of the AFP screening test.

I hadn't wanted to do the birth defects test this time around, but Michael had insisted, straightening his tie and attaching his beeper to his belt. "Why not take full advantage of everything modern medicine has to offer? It's foolish not to." Foolish was often the word that came up before appointments with Naomi. Michael would have preferred going to a regular obstetrician, but I put my foot down about the midwives: I was adamant about having the most natural birth possible, and their track record for having fewer complications and cesareans was much better. Even Michael can't argue against statistics. Facts win fights.

A week ago this argument was abstract, floating around the house in whispers while Sophie slept down the hall. The light from the window was still predawn gray. "But last time it was wrong. It came back positive and we worried ourselves sick for days until the ultrasound showed the mistake. Worried for nothing."

Michael sighed. "It's important to know. If the baby would turn out to have spina bifida, we can be prepared with the whole neonatal surgical team at the birth to try to fix it. Better safe than sorry." He pulled on his crisp white lab coat and kissed my forehead.

I followed him to the bedroom door. "And if it's Down's?"

"That's a big if, Em. Let's wait until the results." And just like that I was getting the test; he was thumping down the stairs.

I take the phone from Michael, and the black receiver is smooth and hard in my fist. My mouth is dry. "Yes?"

"Hi, Emily? This is Naomi."

I swallow. "Hello."

"We have the results of your AFP screening, and they aren't quite normal. They're one in seventy-five."

"What does one in seventy-five mean?" I ask. Michael closes his eyes, and I know that it's bad again.

"It means a one in seventy-five chance your baby has Down syndrome. But remember, there are false positives twenty-five percent of the time. And yours was wrong last time, so let's just schedule an ultrasound and have a look, okay?"

Michael takes the phone and pulls some strings; Naomi will come along to the ultrasound at Michael's hospital tomorrow during lunch so that we don't have to wait and wonder and worry, and so that Michael can come along to see the baby too. With both of us going, we'll have to bring Sophie; there's no time to get a sitter.

He hangs up and puts his hand on my back, rubbing slowly up and down. "At least this way we'll get in there without having to wait a week for the traveling tech to get around to the midwives' office." Michael blows out a deep breath and moves the hair out of my eyes. "Here, play with Sophie. You know it will make you feel better." After a minute in the kitchen Michael hands me our daughter, hands freshly wiped, although they barely needed it. "I'll put your dinner in the fridge for later if you get hungry." Sometimes he does know what I'm feeling.

Sophie clasps and unclasps her fists rapidly, flashing her fingers at me. "Baba, baba!" she squeals and laughs, clapping. She wants to hear about what little babies are like.

"OK, then go get Dolly and we'll talk about babies." I put her down so she can find her doll. Dolly is a small, plush baby doll with a pink sleeper and nightcap from which a few yellow loops of yarn peek out. The knotted top of her cap is dingy gray from being chewed on sometimes. Sophie never goes to sleep without Dolly.

I pull Sophie into my lap on the couch, and she holds Dolly in her lap. She lets Dolly flop over, though, to show me her fingers. "How many fingers does a baby have? One two three four five six seven eight nine ten!" I touch each of Sophie's fingers as I count them off in a voice much more animated than I feel.

Sophie giggles and claps, then kicks her feet. "And how many toes does a baby have? One two three four five six seven eight nine ten!" Her giggles turn into a belly laugh as I tickle each toe.

"And what do big sisters do?" I sing out. Michael was right: Sophie's laugh always makes me feel better. You can't help but smile even just remembering it.

Sophie grabs Dolly and hugs her tight, rubbing her cheek against the doll's cloth one. "That's right: we LOVE them!" And I hug Sophie tight. This is our game.

Sophie wriggles out of my arms and hands me Dolly. I take the doll and make a show of rocking it back and forth and giving it a big kiss, which makes Sophie squeal again.

"MAmama. MAmama."

Sophie has a million ways of saying my name to mean different things. This one means "again." She almost doesn't need more than the four words she knows; I always get her point. Sometimes Michael needs a translation, though.

"Again? Ok!" And we play the baby game five or six more times until she starts to rub her eyes. "Soap time for Sophie!"

I look up and Michael is standing in the doorway of the kitchen watching us, a little sadly. "Can Daddy do bath time tonight?" he asks softly.

"Dada!" Sophie is crawling toward him, definitely tired if she's not on her feet. I'm glad she was agreeable to this change of routine: Michael could probably use a dose of Sophie's laughter too.

I watch the rain travel up the passenger side window in an arc as the car speeds down the highway to the hospital. Everything is gray: car interior, pavement, guardrail, sky. "I'm not sure I want to keep having all these tests."

"Emmie, it's an ultrasound. That's hardly a test, and there's really no risk."

"The risk is that we make a decision because we're scared. That we do the wrong thing. That we—"

"Shh," Michael interrupts, eyes on the rearview mirror. Sophie's asleep.

"I just don't want to worry about this anymore when it's probably wrong," I hiss in a stage whisper.

"That's totally irrational." He glances over and meets my glare. Backpedaling. "I mean, it just doesn't make much sense. The test is what will make us *stop* worrying by showing us conclusively that everything is normal."

"But I thought an ultrasound wasn't conclusive, just another piece of the puzzle."

"True, but an amnio is."

I shudder at how casually he can toss around the idea of a giant, cold needle poking through my stomach and into our baby's cozy nest. I pull the visor down and flip up the cover over the vanity mirror, adjusting it so I can see Sophie in her car seat. "But what will we do if it *is* positive for Down's?" This time my whisper is real; I can barely choke out the sentence.

Michael keeps his eyes on the road. "Em, we've talked about this before. When we thought it would be a problem the last time. Now it should be even more obvious what we'd do, because it's not just us anymore. It wouldn't be fair to Sophie for someone to take away so much of the attention that she should have."

"I just don't think—"

"Emmie, come on. It's just an ultrasound! Why are you so insane about everything this time around? Talk about the second time being different from the first ..."

I bite my lip and look up into the mirror. Sophie's head is hanging to the side; her eyes are closed and her mouth makes a straight little pink line over her chin. She's holding Dolly loosely in her lap. "Because the first time I didn't know what it meant."

Michael is bent over the tech's shoulder, peering at the computer screen. His back is to me and he is quiet.

"Michael, move. I can't see the baby. Can you tell if it's a boy or a girl?" I start to sit up for a better view.

The technician pulls the sensor off my slippery belly and sets it on the desk. "The doctor and midwife will be in to see you shortly." The door clicks shut.

The room is dim so that everyone can read the computer screen images better. When Michael turns to me, I know. "What is it?"

"The neck measurements are off. The doctor will tell us it's consistent with Down's." Michael sighs and sits down on the round leather toadstool that every doctor's office has.

I look to Sophie, who is playing with Dolly in a corner. She bounces her up and down. Dolly, it seems, is learning to walk.

"Now what?"

"An amnio, then we'll know for sure." The midwife and the OB, called in for our now high-risk case, echo Michael's words. The leather-faced obstetrician is a friend of Michael's, and is willing to skip lunch to get our amniocentesis done today.

"Take Sophie out to the lobby."

"Are you sure you want to do it by yourself? I know how you feel about needles ..." Michael looks tired.

"And I don't want her to be the same way, so I don't want her to see my reaction to this. Naomi's here, so I'm not alone." I close my eyes, and swallow the lump in my throat.

I don't open my eyes until the door clicks shut again. The thin little blonde tech is back, opening packages of needles and vials of liquid.

"Just close your eyes and breathe deeply. In and out. In and out." Naomi takes my hand, and it is like the night Sophie was born. But before I close my eyes completely, the doctor turns up the lights and they reflect off the long, silver line of the needle. I breathe.

There is a burning to the side of my bellybutton that Naomi tells me is the anesthesia. Then I feel another sting, and a weird pulling feeling inside me. I can't see it, Naomi is keeping me calm, but I know what it feels like, anesthesia or no. Something is being pulled out of me, slowly.

Back in clothes and shoes, I walk over to Michael and Sophie. I reach for her, but Michael shakes his head. "No strenuous activity for the rest of the day. I'll take Sophie to my mother's so you can rest while I'm at work tonight." Opening the door into the hospital hallway, he looks me in the face. "Are you okay?"

"I guess so. I'll be better when the waiting is over, I think."

I am upstairs in our bedroom cleaning when Michael gets home from work. Day four of waiting, of using housework to keep myself busy whenever Sophie is asleep.

Michael walks to his side of the bed and clears a spot to sit down on. Sophie's laundry is piled all over the rumpled yellow comforter, and he drops fistfuls of tiny socks back into the basket. He sets his watch and beeper on the nightstand and turns toward me.

"How was work?" I ask, reaching for the socks. A mock sigh. "I had these all sorted out, Pigpen." I smile and look up. Michael's haggard face is like a photo negative of a night sky: under his eyes are dark crescent moons in a pale universe. I freeze.

"Jim—Dr. Barton—came by today. He wanted to talk in person about the amnio results. Em, it's Down's." He looks down at his fingers kneading the yellow folds of the comforter like they belong to somebody else.

How nice of Jim to be so sensitive to Michael, to have added the personal touch. I can see them stepping aside into an empty conference room to murmur to each other. Maybe Jim touched Michael's shoulder. All this, while I was scrubbing, dusting, folding, sweeping. Alone.

"Maybe it's wrong. Maybe the test is wrong," I plead with Michael across our bed. I lurch into motion again, pulling the arms of one of Sophie's shirts back and folding it in half. I smooth it flat and grab for another.

"The test isn't wrong." With the palm of his hand, Michael sweeps away the wrinkles he has made. The creases are gone, but he continues the motion, back and forth, staring at the bed.

"But it just doesn't feel—"

Michael is on his feet. He whirls around to face me. "Would you stop it with the feelings already? The test is right. You're wrong. Let it go." His pinched voice finally cracks and he stops.

I fold faster and the stack of pink, yellow, and white onesies grows taller. I breathe through my nose in a hiss.

Michael sighs and his voice comes out softer. "Maybe you were right about the way you felt earlier. You said the pregnancy felt different and were worried about miscarrying. Maybe you were supposed to."

"How come when *you* argue with your so-called anecdotal evidence, it's okay?"

"Emmie, that's exactly my point. You can use intuition or feelings or pangs or whatever you want to call it to argue any side, any point. But you can't argue against the test results." Michael gathers up the rest of Sophie's clothes. "It doesn't take a doctor to see that." He heads for the door, but I grab his arm.

"What happens now? We can't *not* talk about it."

"We did talk about it. The first time. I'll call Dr. Barton and schedule—"

"Michael!" I drop his arm and step back. "It's not that easy. It can't be. It's not just a statistical problem to be solved. It's a—it's *our* baby." Michael's biting his lips white and his eyes are swimming, but I press on. "Our child, and I don't even know if it's a boy or a girl."

Michael places the laundry basket on the floor at the end of the bed and sits down again. "Em, don't make this harder than it already is. If you—I mean, if we—if we knew the sex, we might be too attached to … to do what we need to." Elbows on his knees, Michael makes a steeple around his nose with his hands, thumbs tucked under his chin, eyes looking up at me over the long, slender fingers.

"Too attached? Of course I'm attached. It's our *baby*, Michael." He closes his eyes and I know I should stop, but I don't. "*No* baby would have been as easy or neat as Sophie. So there'll be more crying and more trips to the doctor and more trouble at school. So what? Different isn't bad, it's just different. Go into Sophie's room and watch her breathe while she's sleeping. Would you be able to abort *her*?"

From its place on the nightstand, Michael's watch ticks out several seconds. He drops his hands on his lap, and when he speaks, there is steel in his voice. "Sophie is the one I'm thinking about." He rises. "Don't you see what her life would be like? Always having to wait her turn for just a few seconds of our attention. Needing student loans because all the money went to extra medical care. Living the rest of her life under the burden of having to take over for us when we die. Because that's what will happen, Em. Who do you think will be designated legal guardian in our wills? It's either that or an institution if the baby is low functioning. Is that really what you want? Don't stand there and tell *me* to think of Sophie, when she's the one who will have to take care of her brother for the rest of her life." Michael stops his lower lip from quivering by pulling back the muscles around his jaw. He paws at his eyes, and when he moves his hand away, they look strangled, somehow.

Sophie's brother. So it's a boy. A son, a loss: one that the miracle of medicine will anesthetize away, as if he weren't real. I look at the floor. "I don't want to blame Sophie for this. I don't want to end up resenting her …"

"Then blame me." Michael has been looking out the window into the orange glare of the street lamp. He throws open the window and takes big, heaving breaths of the cold air that rushes in on both of us.

Another white room, dimly lit. Another flimsy, bluish hospital gown and leatherette exam table. "No anesthesia," I tell the tech.

"Are you sure?" she asks. She is a large woman with little pink and red hearts all over her scrubs. "Some women do find it painful."

"I want to feel it. Where is my husband?"

"He's signing some papers, and probably a waiver about the anesthesia. It's not policy for him to be in here, but I guess since he's a friend of Dr. Barton …"

"Fine." I turn away from her to look at the wall. I close my eyes against its whiteness.

We haven't spoken since yesterday afternoon on the way to the first appointment at the clinic. I didn't know you had to go twice; the first time they put in something that feels like seaweed, lumpy and slimy. "It helps with the dilation," Naomi explained in our counseling session.

"Good to see you, Michael. Is your wife ready?" I open my eyes to see the swarthy, mustachioed doctor sit on his toadstool by my feet. I didn't hear Michael come in the room, but he is standing by my head. The tech comes back in the room wheeling a shiny metal tray with a clear glass jar hooked up to a hose. The doctor looks up at Michael and raises his eyebrows. "Are you sure about this, Mike?"

"Em, please let them give you something for the pain. There's no reason to torture yourself." These are the first words Michael has spoken to me all day; they come out in an airy hush.

"No."

When it comes, it is like the wind. The whoosh of the vacuum roars in my ears and takes my breath away, like opening the door into a hurricane. My stomach cramps and heaves; the jar on the tray fills with blood so red it is almost glowing in the fluorescent light of the exam room.

Michael's hands are cold on my cheek as he turns my head away from the cart and toward him, toward the wall. I look up at him and he closes his eyes. "No, Michael," I say. My voice cracks, but I go on. "Someone has to watch."

He opens his eyes slowly and stares over my head to the cart on the other side of the room. His jaw starts working; he is biting the insides of his cheeks. A grimace and a swallow: we are both bleeding. His hand is still on my cheek, keeping me from watching the jar fill with blood and baby.

Sophie is home after a week at her Grammy's, and she has been tearing around all day, pulling toys out of every possible place and strewing them about the house. I have been lying on the couch watching her, getting up to make her snacks when she gets hungry. I keep my eyes closed and doze when I can. The bleeding is almost done, but I am still tired. It reminds me of the weeks after we brought Sophie home from the hospital.

"Nonono."

I open my eyes and Sophie is standing, staring right into my face. I have an afghan scrunched up around my shoulders, but she pulls it down so she can see me better. I'm cold without it. "Yes yes yes. Mommy's tired, Sophie."

Sophie starts flexing her hands over and over as fast as she can, showing me her fingers. "NonoNO!"

"What is it, Soph?"

"NoNO!" Sophie swoops Dolly up from the floor onto the couch and jabs her finger at Dolly's hand, punching into the soft fabric insistently, rhythmically. "NoNO. NoNO."

I look down at Dolly's grayish hand. No NO. One two. Dolly's hand is like a mitten, only the suggestion of a thumb and a hand. Not the ten fingers we had been counting on together before. The game is not the same, and Sophie wails in frustration.

"NoNO. NONO!" Michael would never believe that Sophie can count, but she knows that two is not ten. Sophie continues to push on Dolly's hands until I take it up by the dingy pink nightcap and hide it under the blanket.

The front door creaks open. Flurries blow in with Michael.

Sophie bursts into tears. "Baba! Baba!"

This is too hard. I want to crawl under the mottled old afghan with Dolly and hide. I sit up instead.

Michael drops his overcoat on the easy chair and kneels down in front of the couch and pulls Sophie into a hug. He bounces her up and down until her crying turns into whining for Dolly. "Baba," she hiccups.

I pull Dolly out from the safety of the afghan and hand the toy to Michael. "She wants Dolly," I translate and pull the blanket up around my shoulders like a shawl.

"OK, Sophie, here's your Dolly. What's wrong, baby?"

Sophie starts hitting Dolly's hands again. "BaBA. BaBA. Dada?" She hands Dolly to Michael, looking up into his face with bright eyes.

Michael looks to me in confusion. I explain about Dolly's hands. "Yes Sophie, one two. That's not your fault, sweetie. It's nobody's fault." He glances at me curled in my shroud. "We still love Dolly." Michael rocks Dolly in his arms and kisses its nose. Then he brushes Sophie's hair out of her face and kisses her nose. Sophie laughs and stretches her arms out to receive her baby doll. She crawls away a few paces and bounces Dolly on her lap, squealing and laughing again.

Michael sits down on the couch next to me. He touches my face the same way he touched Sophie's, even though all my hair is back in a ponytail. "How are you feeling today?"

"Okay. Better." I take his hand and pull it into the warmth of the afghan. We stare at Sophie on the rug in front of us. She is starting to roll around on the floor, pausing when Dolly is comfortable under her cheek as a pillow.

"C'mon, Soph," Michael whispers. "Let's go night-night." He scoops her up into a cradle hold and heads for the stairs.

"Wait, Michael." I pick up Dolly and catch up to him at the bottom of the stairs. "You forgot Dolly." But Sophie is already asleep, nestled against Michael's chest.

"Never mind."

I curl back up on the couch with Dolly tucked between my arm and my breast, blanket over just my feet. Michael's footsteps tread softly up the stairs and fade away as he nears Sophie's room. I close my eyes and breathe in Sophie's smell from Dolly's pink cap. I haven't lied to Michael: I am better, but it's still too hard. When I hear Michael's footsteps returning, I put Dolly on the floor, pull the afghan up under my chin, and pretend to be asleep until I really am.

Results

I grip the sharp, plasticky edge in my teeth to get a better hold as I twist and yank at the spot where the wrapper is molded together into a tri-fold. It tastes like the wings they stick in your cheek at the dentist to separate your teeth for x-rays, but those are soft, and this is cutting the roof of my mouth. I shift my weight, bobbing unevenly from my left foot to my right and back again, propelled from some nervous place near my stomach. This might be easier if I didn't have to go to the bathroom so badly: I feel like a little kid. I shift the wrapper edge to spear it with my right eye-tooth and give it one more downward tug. Finally.

The staticky wrapper doesn't want to let go of my hand after the battle, but I manage to shake it off into the trash. Still in my jerking, side-to-side rhythm, I puff out some Lamaze-style breaths to try to calm down as I pop off the white plastic cap and set it on the edge of the sink. I yank down my flannel pajama bottoms and sit on the cold, hard toilet seat, elbows on thighs, and look at the stick. This little plastic wand was pretty expensive, but even so, I was hoping that by now I wouldn't need it, that I would be glad to have traded a little tip money for the relief of an unopened package. But a week's worth of spotless underwear later, here I sit, past the deadline I set and shivering in the bathroom. This is not what I planned to be doing the Friday before midterms in my second-to-last semester.

Exhale.

The directions say to cover the indicator window with my thumb to protect it from the urine stream so the results won't be invalidated by a stray drop or two. It's like holding a toothbrush, except there's a stiff, cottony thing where the bristles would be, and I hold it so it's pointing straight down at the toilet water. Start the urine stream and then move the stick into the stream for five seconds. But the directions also say to face the indicator window away from the urine stream. In the goofy health-class line drawing, it shows the little window facing to the right-hand side on a right-handed woman. The part it doesn't show is how in reality this twists your arm around so your thumb, still on the window, is angled out and your shoulder is rotated in toward your chest in an extremely uncomfortable, marionette sort of way. But it's only for five seconds, so I hold the pose and get ready to pee.

And oh, do I have to go. It says on the package that the test is "Ultra-sensitive! Results in seconds!" and that first morning urine is not really necessary, but that's what I've always heard, so that's what I've got saved up. I drop my head between my arms, chin on chest, and stare between my legs at the clear water in the bowl. Now that I'm thinking about it, it's not so easy, and so I imagine that story about the little boy who fell over the Horseshoe Falls and the hand of God miraculously saved him, with some help from a white guy and a black guy standing by in the crowd … That little boy floats toward the drop, sucked along by millions of tons of water …

One Mississippi.

Two Mississippi.

Three Mississippi.

Four Mississippi.

Five Mississippi.

There's way more than five seconds of pee here, so I maneuver the stick to the side, glad to untwist my arm, and let the rest of the amber liquid in my bladder splash into the toilet. It feels good to let it out, but only for another Mississippi or two, and then the nervous tingle is back and I feel the ghost pee, the phantom urge to go that comes back, even though I know there's nothing left. The tingling feeling grows into a lump that sits in my stomach, heavy and kicking up at my lungs, making it hard to breathe. My hands prick with the beginnings of sweat, and when I think about stopping it, they just get clammier, colder.

Nothing in my body is listening to me.

The directions don't offer any advice about how to wipe with a drippy stick in your hand, so I reach for the cap I left on the sink and put it on, then I put the stick—indicator-side up—back on the sink, which I guess is a cool and undisturbed enough place for the next three minutes. I check my watch, since exact timing is supposed to yield best results.

One hundred eighty seconds.

Commercials take this long, or maybe the loop from the kitchen to the soda fountain and around my section to see how the food is, if anyone needs a refill. This is about how long I wait on hold with the registrar each semester while I wait to type in the codes for courses like "Entrepreneurial Thinking" and "Financial Management for Tourism and Hospitality." It's shorter than the time it took to make my pros-and-cons list about going to grad school. About the same amount of time it took to make and then tear up the pros-and-cons list about getting an apartment with David.

I unravel a nice, thick handful of toilet paper and wipe myself off. Twice. I have three minutes to kill, so I might as well be thorough. I stand up, pull up my now-cold flannels, and press the cold handle to flush the toilet. Sh-fwhoosh. Spin, spin, spin. Gluggle glug glug. Hiss. The water pressure seems low, and maybe this weekend I will check that out before it starts backing up again like it was a month ago. David said he looked at it, that it was fine, but I know he only jiggled the handle, and anyway, he's more of a big-picture, building-the-framework kind of construction guy. He's got a big project this fall, a whole housing development to finish before the snow comes, so he's out the door before the sun comes up, home after it's down. On Saturday he'll want to sleep in and then hit the paints on his new series, "Rage in Reds and Rusts" or something, so that leaves to me the details of keeping this place in working order. David has been putting together a second showing at a small gallery, and the new Applebee's at the mall bought one of his pieces to add "local flavor" to the test-marketed clutter on the walls. He rolls his eyes at the idea of his work collecting grease and dust at a chain restaurant, but I remind him that this is good exposure and could attract more people to the out-of-the-way gallery. He doesn't much care for marketing, and I do not mention that the restaurant sale is his biggest commercial success, something to build on rather than to scoff at. David does not want a manager.

I cinch up the silky red drawstring and make a bow.

One hundred thirty-five seconds.

I could brush my teeth. But that will contaminate the cool, dry, undisturbed place where I put the stick. Besides, it will probably be better if I don't look at it until the three minutes are up, so I don't get nervous or upset before there's any real reason to be. My friends have told me that the sticks show if you're pregnant right away — something like two or three seconds, and if it takes longer than that, you aren't. The leaflet in the box says to give it three minutes, minimum, and no more than ten. I'm not sure who to believe: uterus-equipped women who have been pregnant or guys in lab coats with PhDs.

Standing here staring in the mirror is making me tired. Looking at the purplish smudges and the little lines in the thin skin under my eyes makes me feel even more exhausted than I already am. Without mascara, my eyes look small and faded, and the part that you notice is the half-moon of oxygen-less blood that is stuck near my eyes because my circulation is too slow to push it along to the rest of my face this early in the morning. My eyebrows need tweezing. My split ends need trimming. There's no one to impress at an eight a.m. class, but a little time investment here might help up my tips from the mildly drunk nightcap-and-brownie-sundae crowd. I think David just sees my skin and hair as highlight and shadow, calculating how to mix the colors it would take to get it right if I ever let him paint me.

Seventy-five seconds.

I clasp my nose with my hands prayer-style, with my index fingers pushing up under my brow bone. I close my eyes and rub them at the corners. It feels good to rub my eyes, and I push up along my eyebrows with all the fingers, smoothing out the hairs until I reach my temples, then dragging my hands down the sides of my cheeks. I open my eyes, and I am still in the mirror, with redder eyes that don't seem any more alert or pretty, just blinkier. How much worse would this be with a baby, being up all night on top of classes and working all day?

Sixty-two seconds.

I think the light is buzzing, and it is so quiet that I can hear my watch ticking its feeble little clicks every second. I should go get something to eat, or a magazine to read, or put some slippers on—the veins in my feet are reddish-purple and my skin is cold on the tile floor. I break eye contact with my reflection and turn to the door. I turn back. I just want to look at the stick already and know for sure so I can plan the next month of my life. Even if it's positive, I just want to know. And when I know, then I can tell David, if I need to. But to get him worked up before, maybe for no reason, would be a waste of effort: Why make him crazy? Or mad, or afraid, or whatever he'd be when he stopped slinging paint around the room and getting little multicolored speckles all over my textbooks and notes and the computer screen. This apartment is full of paint, little bits of it everywhere, drips that don't come up because you don't see them until they're dry and stuck-on wherever it is they landed. We'll never get the security deposit back.

Forty-seven seconds.

Forty-seven Mississippis to go. That doesn't seem like much, but looking at the watch face shows three-quarters of the circle left to go for Mickey's contortionist act. He looks very *Saturday Night Fever* right now, with his short, gimpy arm pointed to the floor and the longer one sassily pointing to his imaginary disco ball. He's smiling, I can see, as the back stub of the second hand sweeps to the side and uncovers his little red mouth.

Forty-one seconds.

Maybe I could've told David about the test this morning before he left. I was awake, facing the wall and lying still, waiting for him to lace up his work boots, close the door, and stride down the hall with his heavy, steel-toed steps. I can imagine him wild, causing a scene in the living room, pacing a loop from the fridge to the TV, or throwing down a freshly stretched canvas and prying open big cans of paint, turning his nervous energy into giant smears of color. But really, that is the old David, the one who used to beg me to let him paint me, to cover me over in paint in layers and swirls until my skin and hair would be caked in the thick mask of his version of me. He has stopped asking for this, and his manic energy, the rhythms of his lean legs and arms, are unleashed only over the canvas. For me he is quiet, in profile mostly, as we watch TV or read side by side in bed. I probably could have told him and been met with calm, all the silence and breathing room I thought I wanted. Now I'm not so sure: the hush has a weight of its own.

Thirty-six seconds.

Thirty-six Mississippi.

Thirty-five Mississippi.

Thirty-four Mississippi.

I lean my back against the door, and it thuds shut: ker-thunk, between me and the mess David has left behind. There are no windows in here, but the sun is probably working its way up, shedding a gray half-light over all of our mixed-up things: computer and canvas, brushes and books. This is no place for a baby, our cheap little studio apartment that never really got the homey touches we promised ourselves when we found it together. Two summers ago it seemed exciting to arrange all our things, to pull them out of boxes labeled "Nicole" and "David" and see how they looked in new groupings, but now it's messy, packed too-tight. Where would we deal in a whole extra person, something that wouldn't be mine or his, but some uncategorizable combination of us?

Thirty-two Mississippi.

Thirty-one Mississippi.

Thirty Mississippi.

This is a milestone—only a half-moon left to go. I'm sure I could probably just look at it now, but I've come this far following the directions just right, so I might as well see it through. And I want to give it as much time as I have to show up, just in case it's positive. Sometimes there's not enough of the hormone to show up right away in the urine, and you could be pregnant and not know because the test would be a false negative. They say that it's much more likely to get a false negative than a false positive.

If it is negative, a real one, I could just sink back into the way things are. But if it's positive, even after all my planning? Then it's another list of pros and cons, weights and measurements and calculations. More rearranging of things, to see if there is a combination that fits a baby into grad school and building savings and finding a new place, a career, working my way up until I've done all things I promised myself I would do. This is not how I had pictured it. I can't even visualize where we would put a crib that it could stay clean and safe. Then there are the hazier, more distant parts of the list: a wedding, maybe, and a house, and traveling. If it's positive, then I cut and paste these things to see if they all fit on the same page, working in David's things the best I can. Or figuring out where to make cuts, which things get deleted: mine or his? Time or money? Quality of life or an actual life? David would say to relax, to paint it in: he never removes anything he doesn't like from his work, but just keeps adding color in layers until he's satisfied. He says that the paint hidden underneath isn't gone, but adds to the final version. I pretend I can see it, the blue splash under all those reds and browns, but I can't, not once it's buried.

Twenty-two seconds.

Maybe I could run and get my robe. It's freezing in the bathroom, and that might take up just the right amount of time here at the end so I can look right at it when I get back. I could get my slippers too, and be comfortable for this. If I run, it wouldn't take more than a few seconds, and I wouldn't miss anything except having to listen to the light buzz, which hasn't stopped, and probably means the bulb is going. This weekend is going to be all about fixing up the bathroom.

Eighteen seconds.

Do I still have time to run to my room? I don't think being a little late would matter, because the directions say you can let it go for as long as ten minutes. Does it self-destruct after that? Does anything self-destruct, just implode and disappear, or do you have to do something to it to make it go away?

Fifteen seconds.

I open the door and feel the warmer air on my face. I close the door again, and it makes a breeze that chills me. I don't think there's enough time. Come on, come on already.

I'm shifting my weight again, one hip jutting out and then the other.

Ten seconds.

Nine seconds.

I reach over to the toilet lid and drop it shut. I sit, and the plastic lid is not quite as cold as the enameled seat was two minutes and fifty-one seconds ago. Legs crossed, hands tucked flat against each other between my thighs, the foot in the air taps uncontrollably at nothing.

Seven seconds.

Taptaptaptaptaptaptaptap.

Six seconds.

They say the foot-shaking thing is a sign of the little bit of autism that we all have. Autistic people just have more symptoms.

Four seconds.

Come on, Mickey.

Three seconds.

I wrap the autistic foot tight around my other leg so my legs are crossed at the knees and clamped at the ankles.

Two seconds.

It feels weird to stop the tapping.

One second.

I exhale in a lippy fffffffff sound, unwrap my legs, and stand up. I wipe my hands on my pajama pants. I reach toward the cool, dry place on the sink. After all this, I'm not sure I want to look. Something is coming, will wedge its way into my life and change my plans, no matter what the results are. I want to close my eyes for just one more second of the way things were, when the apartment was clean and new and we couldn't wait to fill it with the chaos of our things and our bodies jostling into each other, combining. But it's already gone.

Exhale and examine.

There, in the plastic window the size of my pinkie nail, is one magenta line, wettish-looking, like it could bleed out fatter across its white background. One line.

A negative.

I squint and look closer, checking for even the faintest tinge of pink, a hair's width of a line in the space where it's supposed to be. One line, alone on its side of the window. I could check again before the ten minute deadline to be sure, but I've done everything right, and this is my answer. I shroud the test stick in a length of white toilet paper, carefully. The wand freefalls into the trash and lands in a hush among crumpled tissues and dental floss.

Out of the bathroom the rest of the apartment is light, and I am untethered, surrounded by airy space. I don't know what time it is, and the day could be getting away from me or slowing down. The floatiness is too much, so I crawl back into bed. In the rush before the test, I had thrown the blankets back wildly, and now the sheets are cold, all the body heat from David and from me has dissipated into the room. I pull them back up to my chin and stare at the ceiling over my side of the bed, waiting to be warm again.

The light, the space: Everything in here feels too far apart, the way a fever feels when you're a little kid. I want to go back to sleep, but it's too bright, and something is missing. I should be relieved, dancing around the place or humming while I clean up and get ready for class, but my stomach is fluttery under my ribs. A phantom, left-over feeling of something that was never there to begin with.

How many Mississippis until it goes away?

I am glad that the test is hidden, that David won't see it if he takes out the trash. I don't want him to find it, because anything I say after that he wouldn't hear, would blame on the baby. Or the not-baby. And anyway, this is something that was mine, was kept clean for a while out of the paint and the jumble of all our stuff. It filled me up, and I hadn't realized there was room for it until it was gone. Now I am doubly empty.

My throat tightens. I miss this thing that was never inside me, that kept me company while I thought about my pros-and-cons list, and how things might be different if I could arrange them just right. But the tiny, fleshy streak of color I could see for a moment has been painted over, flushed out by reds, and then covered over again by the grays and glarey whites of the daylight streaming through the apartment.

September Air

My eyes are shut to the white light of day in the windows. I press my face a little farther into the cushion. It is not my pillow, but instead the tweedy arm of the sofa. I shift slightly, and there is suddenly a cool spot on my breast, a dampness exposed.

Riley.

When I look, I am relieved to see that he is asleep, face tilted up to the light in that raised-eyebrow way that his sister also had, looking more alert and intelligent asleep than awake. He gives two little close-mouthed sucks, and sighs jaggedly. Still asleep, even without his human pacifier now. My shirt is still hiked up, and I don't know how long I've been sleeping or when he stopped nursing, but he seems comfortable. I would love to turn over, to adjust, but I pull my arm in a little tighter around him to make another inch of space between him and the sofa's edge.

I close my eyes again.

In college I had bouts of insomnia, tossing and turning all the things on my to-do list around in my head and watching the red digital numbers on the alarm clock silently count through the hours. I don't remember what this felt like; I have become a master at falling asleep, hard, in just a minute or two, and snapping out of it just as quickly. I am right on the edge of falling off into that place where you know for just a flash that you *are* asleep, and there it is: Thu-thud. Thu-thud. Sam is pushing on her bedroom door, leaning into it with her bottom and then releasing it. I hold my breath and try to relax against it, hoping it will subside, but it gets gradually louder until it is full-out banging. My body is awake, tensed, even though I am trying not to be behind my eyes.

I slide my hand under Riley's fuzzy, dark head and hold him steady while I place him in his vibrating seat. I hold my breath as I slide my arms out from under him and switch it on. He doesn't move, and I sprint upstairs to stop the noise.

"Samantha Janine!" I push the door open quickly. "Stop banging right now."

She has run over to her big girl bed and whirls around. "I mall done!" She smiles, big and dimply, and I relax in spite of myself. Her dark hair is wild, all tangled and teased from her nap. She walks to me leading with her belly, chin tucked in to her chest and eyes looking up coyly through dark lashes. When she bumps me, she throws her arms around my legs and crushes her head into my pelvis, where it can fit again. She leans back to look up at me, using my thighs for balance. "I want O's."

I tilt my head and raise an eyebrow.

"*Please* mayhaveO's?" she corrects herself. "And when Daddy comes home, we will have a *cookie*. I will have choc'late, and Daddy will have plain."

"And what kind of cookie will Mommy eat?" I'm not sure we even have any cookies; Jake probably took the last ones for breakfast in the car.

"No, you don't have a cookie, Mommy. Jus' *Daddy*."

After a too-late trip to the potty and a new pull-up she is buckled into her booster seat and is chattering away at the kitchen table with a red plastic bowl full of dry Cheerios. I am about to make myself a sandwich, but she is banging on the table. "I mall done!"

The Cheerios have not been touched, except for the handful that have been pushed out of the bowl onto the table. "Sam, you are not all done. You need to eat your O's."

"But I don *wan*'um." She slides the bowl away and looks up to me with wrinkled brow and pursed lips. "I wan'ed *sauce*."

"You would like to have some applesauce instead? First eat your O's and then you can have some applesauce." I force this to come out nicely; it sounds high pitched and false in my ears. I feel the prick of adrenaline tickling under the tip of my sternum, starting to tingle down my arms. I take a deep breath and force it back down. I huff out that air and drop my shoulders, flex my hands open hard. I turn back to the counter and finish putting my sandwich together. I haven't eaten since Riley's pre-dawn feeding, and I notice all at once how hungry I am.

I sit down at the table with Sam, who is picking Cheerios out of the bowl one by one. "Mommy, this is a

O." She pops it into her mouth and smiles, chewing. "And *this* is a O. And this is a other O." She talks and talks and talks; I nod and smile and chew. When Riley wakes up crying I bring him to the table and balance him on my arm; he sucks down his lunch while I finish mine with my free hand. When my arm gets tired I cross my leg underneath it and use my knee for leverage, so a different part of me is uncomfortable for a while.

After the first five minutes of Riley nursing, I have a little bit of a sinking feeling, like nestling backwards into a pile of propped up pillows, the way I used to settle in on a drizzly day with a new book. I feel that way even in the awkward positions we sometimes find ourselves in, like alcohol without the buzz, with just the disconnect from what I'm seeing. From this watery distance it is easy for me to leave the edge out of my voice and automatically inject the bright "Ohs" and the "Wows" and the "Great jobs!" into Sam's babble.

I am used to eating with my lunch balanced on my knees, in slightly tensed and strange poses. Those lunches were take-out salads on benches by fountains or under skylights in mid-Atlantic malls, surrounded by people strolling from place to place, or walking fast and talking faster on cell phones, all making a murmur hovering around me at a distance. I used to be a merchandise rep for a designer clothing line, work that had me traveling to regional retailers and tweaking their displays, discussing their needs and how the lines were working for them. I dressed tall, silent, motionless mannequins in new arrivals.

I got to wear a lot of those clothes and meet a lot of people. Shallow retail people, I thought at the time, people who didn't read good books. Breathing in the chlorine air around those fountains, I would count the glints of copper and silver on the pale blue tiles and wonder what wishes were attached to them.

"Mommy, I mall done." I look over to Sam's bowl, which is empty, but there is a small mound of cereal on the table next to the bowl.

"You still have the ones on the table to finish before you get your applesauce." I point to them.

"Mommy! Those are *Kelsey's* O's." Kelsey is Sam's new imaginary friend, and she has been visiting us over the last two weeks, mostly at meals and bedtimes. Kelsey is two, almost three, and likes to do everything that Sam likes to do. "Please mayhavesauce now?"

Riley is beginning to doze again, so I don't want to argue. "Applesauce in a bowl or on a plate?"

"Mmm ... maybe I want crackers."

"Sam." I'm trying to have just the right tone here, gentle but not too lenient, firm but not too mean. The way that young, blonde elementary school teachers talk to their charges in romantic comedies before being whisked off the playground by the leading man.

The phone rings and I put down the last corner of my sandwich, clamp Riley closer to my breast, and pick it up in the next room. "Abby, we did it!" Jake's voice is full of energy, slightly breathless. Stretched into a smile you can hear.

"That's great. So it all went off?" Riley is arching his back and twisting in my arm. He needs my two hands to prop him up straighter; I need one for myself to hold the phone. One of us will have to be uncomfortable. I wedge the phone between my ear and shoulder and sit him up straight while I twist to hold everything in balance.

"… loved it, and we got a three-region deal instead of just the trial. Can you believe it?" I missed some of the details about the suits and the projections and the contracts. Riley's eyes are wide and dark as he scans the room. A thin tether of drool connects his milky lip to my shoulder.

"Wow. Great job, Jake."

"Mommy, *Kelsey's* all done too!"

"So hey, listen, we were probably gonna go out and celebrate after we wrap a few things up here. Is that okay?" I can hear that Jake has pushed a little closer to the phone, turned away from the bustle in the background. I can picture the high fives and the email clicking out of wires and walls like lightning, flashes zipping along thin, electric lines and connecting to other flashes, on and on across offices across the city, filaments holding them together. "I mean, how was your day so far?"

I tell him how many times Riley ate, and for how long; which cartoon Sam watched and how she had a time-out for throwing a matchbox car; how Kelsey is still here and that now she shares Sam's food. At least I think these things happened today, and not yesterday or the day before.

His "Ohs" and "Wows" come into the mouthpiece at an angle, and I hear the hiss of space. "Um, okay, so it's good? It's okay if I come home late?"

I know he doesn't know how long he will stay out, so I don't ask. He shouldn't have to ask permission, but he should ask how I feel; I'm not his mother but I am a mother now: this is the DMZ of our relationship, where we tiptoe cautiously and are careful not to catch ourselves on barbed fences. "It's fine. They've been pretty good today." This has no meaning, really, neither the truth nor a lie. We say goodbye and hang up; the filament snaps out of tension and Jake is floating away, receding back into handshakes and the smell of coffee and Xerox toner. Riley puts a fist in his mouth, breaking the shiny line of drool.

After hand wipes and mouth wipes and a diaper for Riley, we finally stumble out of the front door and into the sunshine. It is clear, and the afternoon light makes everything as sharp and primary as one of Sam's picture books that teach words for everyday things: blue sky, green grass, red flowers, yellow house. The air has finally caught up to the calendar, and all at once I realize that it is September for real, not just in name. The sun is still warm, but the air is cool and dry. I close my eyes and feel the breeze in my nose and across my face, filling both sides of my skin. There is a ripply wave in my chest, fluttering behind my ribcage, and I have an urge to buy colored folders and loose leaf paper, ball point pens and highlighters, and a backpack with lots of zippers and pouches, all ready to be filled with just the right thing. Days broken down by subject and sorted into specialized compartments, clean and neat, and still new. This is what the rest of the world has been doing while I have been inside.

I close the gate behind us and we make our way to the park by the river. Sam is sitting up front, bouncing her head on the green nylon sling of the somewhat rickety umbrella stroller. Next is Riley, fastened against my chest in his faded black carrier. He is still too small to face forward, so his cheek is on my chest and he has pulled his arms in from their slots to curl into his ribs. His legs bounce in rhythm with my steps, and his knees push slightly into my stomach on the beat. This is almost like having him back inside me again, curled and kicking, but with his weight on the opposite side of my skin. This is the only time I can remember what it really felt like to be pregnant, and the feeling is gone as soon as I tune into it. It shimmers on the air just out of my reach, surrounding me but no longer a part of me.

I push everyone along from behind, and Sam talks about the boats and the fish and the trees and the squirrels as we wind along the river path. This really is a beautiful day for a walk, and I am enjoying it even with the extra freight. When we reach the slides, Sam jumps out and runs, and I sit down heavily on a bench, glad to release some of the strain of the shoulder straps. There are other mothers here, in slim-fitting jeans and ballet flats, carrying shoulder bags full of juice boxes, goldfish crackers, sunscreen, diapers and wipes. They are properly equipped. Sam gallops back to me, bareheaded and uncombed, and grabs my hand.

"You take Kelsey. I'm playing with that girl now." She points to a thin, freckled girl in a pink sundress and runs back to the slides again, hand in hand with her new and temporary friend. The adult version of the freckled girl walks over to them, puts some sunscreen on her daughter, and kneels down in front of Sam. Sam shakes her head and points to me. I wave, and the other mom waves back. Sam hates sunscreen, and the greasy struggle to protect her is one I reserve for the beach and the very hottest of days. The woman points to the bottle and then to Sam, miming her willingness to cover my daughter too, but I shake my head no. I add a carefree, loose-wristed sideways wave to lighten my response, to show that I've already taken care of this. Not to worry. The mom sees over Sam's shoulder that another freckled kid is grabbing fistfuls of sand and squeezing it over his head, where it cascades down his smooth hair and over his face. Into his eyes. The mom jumps up and runs over to save the boy from himself.

I let out my breath and am glad she is busy. I don't want to talk about formula versus breast milk and *Baby Einstein* and preschool. I move into the shade and watch Sam play, watch a sailboat float by on the river, watch the light turn a little more golden and the shadows of the maple trees stretch across the mulch under the swings. The other mothers pack up their bags and their children and head down the path to the Wetherbee School; an empty yellow bus rumbles past in a cloud of diesel. Soon the sidewalks will be filled with children laughing and prancing and swinging their backpacks at each other, shoes still squeaky-new.

Sam squats in the mulch and jumps up, reaching for the sky. She is smiling, and I can see the dimples in her cheeks even from my seat under the tree. She waves to me and calls out, "Mommy, look at *me*! I jumping *so big*!" She jumps again, and when I applaud, she claps along with me.

"Great job, Sammy! That's really good jumping!" She jumps again and again, making her way across the open space between the jungle gym and the slides. In the warm sunlight Sam's dark hair looks reddish, and her smooth skin takes on the golden glow that you usually only see in the types of movies that look at the Depression with nostalgia. I wish I had a video camera to save just a piece of this, to catch her in motion in the changing light. In profile Sam looks thinner, much older than she is, and I get a sense of the woman she might become: focused vivacity, a smiling dynamo. Tiring, she flubs a jump and lands on all fours in the scratchy mulch. She turns to look at me, unsure whether to laugh or cry, and she is two years old again. I wave and nod vigorously, showing my biggest smile and my widest eyes. "You're okay! Just brush off the dirt!" She hits her brown knees with her hands a few times, checks her palms, and runs away past the baby slides to climb to the top of the big, echoing, tubular one.

Sam goes up the ladder and down the biggest slide a few more times, then wanders around the sandbox, looking a little bored and a little lost now that the playground is empty. Riley shifts, and it is time to go before he wakes up squawking for milk. "Sammy, come on! Let's go!" My voice stretches out on the air and sounds cheerful, genuine.

Sam plods over slowly, but climbs into her stroller without complaint. We agree to walk past the flower house and the big rock on the way home, so I push the stroller across the street. When the stroller hits the street, Sam is wailing, squeezing tears out of the corners of her eyes in big drops. When we get to the other side I kneel down clumsily, off-balance with Riley strapped to me, and ask her what is wrong. "Mommy Mommy Mommy" she sobs out, hiccupping the breath on its way back in. When she breathes deeply enough to speak again, she cries, "Where's my Kelsey?"

"She's right here with us, ready to go home and eat supper," I say. Whenever Kelsey is with us, she is right next to Sam.

"No! You have to hold her *ha-and*. You have to hold her hand to cross the street!" Sam is moaning now, absorbed in the rhythm of her crying. I silently push the stroller back across the street where I have left Kelsey stranded. I swipe at the air where her hand might be.

"Here she is. All better!"

"No, I want Kelsey to sit with *me*." And we are off again, Sam's breathing still ragged and Riley's too, in the effort of waking up and trying to lift his heavy head off my chest. He starts to make his hungry cry, the grinding sound of an old-time fire truck from down low in his throat. I feel conspicuous in the empty street with their cries surrounding me, and I push faster to get home before the school kids break free from their classrooms.

Back at home Riley is fed while Sam and Kelsey watch *The Lion King*. Again. This is not what I would choose for myself, although I do enjoy the opening scene where all the animals celebrate the birth of Simba. The elephants and giraffes and hippos are joyful in their variety: primal chaos rendered as fable. As the movie goes on, though, I get bored, and after I switch Riley to my other breast, I close my eyes. Maybe I am dozing, maybe I am thinking, but Riley is asleep again, and I should fold the laundry. I place him smoothly, carefully in his swing, switch it on and give a little push. The click-clock sound of the swing is rhythmic, and as I pull tiny onesies and socks from the laundry basket I try to become absorbed in the activity. Zen and the Art of Folding Clothes, the only way to really enjoy and give meaning to the act. Smooth, fold, stack. Again. My laundry rhythm falls in with the sounds of the swing, but the rhythm of my breath pushes against all this, neither hard nor soft, but there. My arms and legs are heavy, but the finger- and toe-tips tingle and try to move without permission. I am thirsty, standing here trying not to think about all these things that want me when I just want myself. Folding clothes to put them in drawers is not the same as folding them for display. Neither satisfies: clothing in drawers is neat but unappreciated; clothing on display tables is fingered and stroked but left in a confused heap.

Once, during the busy season, Jake came to the mall to surprise me for lunch. I was surrounded by tangles of chic grays and sophisticated earth tones, clothing spilling out of boxes and falling in silky ripples across the tile floor. I was pregnant with Sam but still working, no longer nauseated but still small enough to maneuver lightly between the shiny racks of dresses and blouses. When Jake asked me what I wanted, I looked around and said, "This, all of this, to be organized and packed away, and for nobody to touch it for a while. For people to take a day off from needing stuff so it can stay under control. I just want it to be done." I looked up at Jake, his lip pursed and head tilted, as if to see me from a different angle. He had only meant to ask what I wanted for lunch, but he stepped into the pile of clothing and started folding. Soon we had a silent system, like the way we used to do the dishes or split the dusting and vacuuming. I can't tell if this was really the last time we had lunch in a restaurant, or if we used to take our afternoon freedom so for granted that we didn't bother to remember these moments of just us. This is the only one I remember.

Sam's movie hasn't even gotten to the sad part yet when she picks up some of the clothes I've already folded, shakes them out, and tries to fold them again on her chest, imitating my stance.

"Sam." My voice must be too loud, too brittle, because her lower lip pokes out a bit.

"But I wan'ed to help you." She looks sad.

I do not have the words to explain to her that she is not helping me, so I fall back on distraction. "Why don't we play Bunny House instead?" She pulls out the plush bunny dolls and their furniture, and takes the role of the Mommy Bunny. The Mommy Bunny tells the other bunnies what to do: now you wake up, now you eat food, now you play, now you brush teeth, now you sleep. My job is to make Brother Bunny go through all the motions, jump through all the hoops. I am bored of this game long before Sam is, and I can't make myself focus on it for long.

"No, Mommy, you have to put Bunny in *bed* now." Eat, play, bed. Again. A nervous shiver runs down the veins in my arms and I stand up quickly, stepping back from the scene and from Sam. "Mommy! I not mall done!" She isn't done with the game, but for me the repetition has ground down the edges and brushed away the shine. I pull Kelsey out of the air to take my place while I make dinner.

When Sam was a baby and Jake and I still split all the cooking, on my nights I enjoyed making something semi-exotic, inspired by our favorites from the little Thai or Indian places we could still manage to get to, or maybe from a glossy magazine recipe. At dinner parties and Sunday brunches our friends thought this was so wonderful, so progressive: "You're so lucky to have a husband who helps out!" I never saw our division of labor as charitable so much as fair, natural, so I could only smile and nod vaguely at their surprise. Since Riley was born, I do all the cooking, and the dishes afterwards. I know if I ask, Jake will reach into the pile of dishes and stand beside me, silent and industrious, but I can't ask. This is what I do, and I need to do it carefully, competently. Alone. I don't love these things, these heaps of plates and clothes and toys that grow and shrink but never disappear, but they are a part of me, just like Sam and Riley and Jake and the plaster walls that hold us together.

"Mommy, I want Daddy to put me to bed." We are eating forkfuls of macaroni and cheese: Sam slowly as she balances the food on her fork, me quickly so I can finish it and get the bath ready, pushing the bedtime ritual along before Riley wakes up for his last feeding. In another two hours they will be asleep, and the house will be, at last, quiet.

I explain that tonight Daddy is working late, and this is met with narrowed eyes and hardened jaw. Anger is almost frightening in a two-year-old in its speed and intensity. Her face turns red. "NO! I want DADDY!" She punctuates this with the bang of her fork.

Of course she wants Daddy; he doesn't wash her hair in the bath. He thinks that I don't know this, but I can smell the difference in the morning when she hugs me. Jake skips it because he can't stand to make her cry when the soapy water runs in her eyes. "Daddy isn't here."

I know this will make her cry, and it does. I walk away, clearing the plates streaked with cold orange cheese. She yells out sharp cries, gravelly in her anger as her throat constricts: "Daddy Daddy Daddy Daddy."

When I come back into the kitchen my movements are crisp and sharp, like an emergency room receptionist. I unbuckle her, lift her out of the seat, and carry her to the bathroom on my hip. I have shocked her into a quieter cry, and her shouting has turned to "hnnn hnnn hnnn" in moans as she tries to get her breath. I undress her while the tub fills and drop her down into the bath without testing the water. "Is it hot?"

She looks at me, eyes still pink around the edges, and shakes her head. She sniffles and says, "I don't wan' the water in my eyes," and she closes them, sitting very still. Her shaky breaths gradually smooth out as I wash her face, her hair, her back. I let her do her legs on her own while I go get her pajamas. In her room I stop, open the window a bit, and watch as the sheer white curtain hem sucks into the crack. I open it wider, and it feels like fall slicing through the steamy air from her bath. It is dark. I breathe. Later, after Sam has fallen to sleep, I will sit on the edge of her rumpled, toy-filled bed and breathe again, this time loving her close warm scent, sweat and baby shampoo filling me up. I will watch her eyes flutter in dreams, watch her curl into herself with her arm around whatever animal she loves best tonight, and love her like that: reflexively, possessively. The way I wish I could love her in the busy glare of day.

Sam is cooperative, pliable, for the rest of our bedtime routine: dry off, potty, brush teeth. When she turns off the water I hear the quiet beginnings of Riley's hunger cries. They are low now, still sleepy, but I don't have long before he is screaming.

I rush Sam into her room and read *Brown Bear, Brown Bear, What Do You See?* as fast as I can. She turns the pages, and there is a pause between the last word leaving my lips and her savoring the rhymes and the bright pictures, and then reaching out to pincer-grasp the corner of the thick cardboard page. In each silent, dead spot, I tense my leg to keep from tapping my foot with impatience. I swallow saliva that fills my mouth. I feel my stomach flutter, and my breasts fill and tingle with milk. I hear Riley's cries cross the threshold from shushable to desperate to shrieks of anguish. Turn the page, read, repeat. Each time it is harder for me to push down the thing that is growing in my chest, lifting into my neck and down my arms to my hands.

Last page, and I tuck in and kiss and kiss again. Repeat for Kelsey. Turn on the nightlight and the music box. This part used to be drawn out, carry the weight of ritual for us, but I have skimmed it lightly tonight. I close her door and hear the full force of Riley's needs echoing down the hall. I sprint soundlessly toward him.

When I jiggle off the buckles that hold him in the swing, Riley throws himself forward so hard that I almost drop him. His new power has scared him, and he screams tearlessly. He cries so hard that he hiccups on my breast and can't keep his latch. Milk is running down my side, but I only feel it as it cools and evaporates on my skin. Riley pounds on my chest and digs his tiny, razor-sharp fingernails into my side. He is sucking me in and pushing me away at the same time. I close my eyes, and tense my arms around him. I arch my back slightly, but he hangs on.

A fast sucking pop and he has let go, leaving my nipple red and shiny in the air. He is shivering on his outward breaths, and I make shushing sounds in his ear, hissing ocean pulling back from the sand, or amniotic fluid on his skin. I rock him, swaying, not loose and bouncy, but long, smooth swings through the air. I imitate a safe place for him the best I can, pretending that I am still a womb for him. His eyes droop. I keep him moving back and forth, at arm's length, as I take some slow steps toward his room. It is a precarious dance.

I am breathing heavily, panting as if I have been running, and I put him down in his crib. I place my hand on his stomach and wait for him to relax, to be asleep and not notice that I'm leaving. My arm is straight and stiff, and I am afraid I am pushing on his soft belly too hard, so I ease back. He whimpers. I drop my shoulders, let the natural weight of my arm rest on him without pushing, without pulling back.

He is quiet again, and I don't know how long I stand watching his eyes flutter and dart behind the lids. I lift my hand and tiptoe a step closer to the door, reaching through the dusk for the shiny brass knob. He erupts, a cry that starts low in his belly and moves through his throat to a siren scream. I feel my hand clench around his soft skin and from the pit of my stomach growls my own siren. My ears are hot. The adrenal rush that I have been able to choke back before gushes out of me, racing down to my toes and out to my fingertips. Every hair is raised, every muscle tingling, and I look at my hand on Riley. His eyes are squeezed tight, his mouth is open, but I don't hear him anymore. Darkness is pushing in on the edges of my vision, and I can see only Riley, tunneled in front of me and framed by white specks that dance around my eyes. I want to hit him, to push through his belly and feel it balloon out around my hand, hot and soft. I want him to hurt so that I can stop.

The white spots flash at once and I blink, and snatch my hand back from Riley. I am holding my breath, and run for the window. I throw it open and thrust my hands to push the screen out. The screen doesn't move, and my arms go through, scratching from my wrists to my elbows. I gasp in the cold air, gulping and wiping my sweaty face against the screen. Riley is safe and I am the one bleeding, tiny but real, thin lines of red cooling my skin in the autumn night.

The screen against my cheek smells like rain and car exhaust. My arms are still tensed and reaching, and finally I let them relax into the broken bits of mesh. Out in the street, a pair of headlights flashes over the rise and blind me until they pass our house. When I can see again, my head is pounding and my legs are shaking, almost jumping, like they did when I came down off the rush after Riley was born, when they twitched and leapt in the bed like live things while the doctor tried to stitch up the place where I had torn. He had a nurse press my knees into the bed, but they would not be stopped, and he had to wait until their weird, possessed dance was done. He sighed in impatience, but I watched, fascinated by what my body could do without my permission. In the end, Riley was the one who made it all stop, holding me in his gaze and subduing me when I finally got to hold him, wrapped tight in the hospital-issue swaddling. I remember feeling what power I had over him, so tiny and helpless bound up in my arms, needing me for everything. But it's this needing that I can't control, can't shut off. It's everywhere, all around me like the air. I don't get to take a break from breathing, even though most of the time I don't even notice I'm doing it. Only sometimes, when it burns after holding my breath so I can feel it again, like the first time, like when Sam and then Riley gasped in and then spit out their first helpless bleats.

And it does burn as I suck in the metallic night air. I look at my arms, pilloried in the screen, white in the light from the passing cars. They are thin and, I realize, cold. There is no one to tell about this, not even Jake: This is not the kind of thing that the moms in the park discuss. This is what we don't tell, for shame or for pride. Or for fear. I open my mouth, but only squeeze out a strangled squeak. It dies on the wind.

I don't know what I will tell Jake about the screen, or even how soon he will notice it. He will come home tired from the week of extra hours at work. I will pull myself back inside, scratching my arms open again on the jagged edges. I will clean up the mess, put the house back together again, and the blood will dry. I will listen to Riley cry himself to sleep, and when he is quiet I will crawl into bed and curl up under the covers in the dark, ready to consume sleep like a meal so I can have the stamina to do better tomorrow. Tomorrow, when I will want to read to Sam when she climbs into my lap and lifts my arm up around her small, hot shoulders. Tomorrow, when I pull Riley's slick-soft baby hair to my cheek and nuzzle across his head, breathing in his milky scent. Tonight I will fall asleep listening for my children's breathing, their growing, imperceptible but real. Later, when Jake crawls into bed and eases his tan arm around me, I don't know if he will feel the crustiness of my arm and wonder what caused my wounds, or if he will think fleetingly that my skin has dried out this fall, that I have aged, and then fall heavily asleep on the pillow beside me.

Afterword

In a masterstroke of poor timing, I decided to work on my master's degree during precisely the five-year span when I was pregnant and nursing my babies. I managed to squeak in just one class in which my body and brain were all my own, but by the final weeks of my second class, I was using a rubber band to expand the buttonhole on my jeans and marveling at my voluptuous new bra size.

From then on, all of the writing I did—whether an academic deconstruction of Shakespeare's comedies or scratching out my own stories and poems—happened during a time when my body was doing extraordinary work of its own. Always hungry, always thirsty, and nearly always tired, I kept plugging away at creating something on the page while the rest of me worked at building baby parts or making milk.

Just when I was finished nursing the first one, I signed up for a second round. My younger one was weaned as I began work on my final project, so my most fertile period of writing neatly bookended the most fertile years of my reproductive life, too. They say to write about what you know, and plans I had to work on a novella about an antiheroine who crashed cars on purpose and had an affair with her student fell by the wayside as I found myself coming back, again and again, to the most singular experience of my life: carrying another human around in my body.

How could it be any other way?

In her book *The Mask of Motherhood: How Becoming a Mother Changes Everything and Why We Pretend It Doesn't,* journalist Susan Maushart maintains that early pregnancy is often difficult for women because they are "left stranded" without "witnesses" to the physical and emotional exhaustion of hosting a growing fetus.[1]

Because the physical strain of early pregnancy is not obviously on display the way it is in the third trimester and during childbirth, it does not garner the same respect—or even acknowledgement—by society at large: "there can be no audience … The drama is entirely offstage."[1]

This unwitnessed drama has been performed a million times across history by women who have been actively discouraged from telling that story. That's an awful lot of unsung heroines muddling through without a model. As Maushart eloquently describes it, this gap on the library shelves leaves a woman to fend for herself "like a new Eve, making it up as she goes along."[1]

And make it up we do. Despite having all the advice in the world just a keystroke away, there's a real loneliness to pregnancy. If there's one thing that unites the characters in these stories, it's their isolation from the outside world as they focus on the drama playing out in within their own bodies. There's Nicole, literally alone as she waits to find out the results of her pregnancy test, and Abby, who struggles to get through another day alone with her very young children while her husband is at work. Emmie is isolated because she's in conflict with her husband about terminating her pregnancy, and Julia is left alone by Rick after the delivery—though she has the glimmer of an opportunity to reconnect with her mother at the end.

So many women doing their work alone. This may not be how women throughout history have done it, but it's par for the course in twenty-first-century America. We don't have a village to help us keep an eye on the baby while we catch a nap, or a live-in lactation specialist to talk us through that first terrifying week at home. (I would have settled for a relative closer than a six-hour drive away.)

What we do have is an impossible standard and a generous salting of guilt.

In *The Mommy Myth: The Idealization of Motherhood and How It Has Undermined Women*, Susan Douglas and Meredith Michaels explore the rise of the celebrity mom. The image of the beautiful celebrity mother who has work and career perfectly balanced presents a one-sided portrait of motherhood that "banishe[s] all ... negativity: No ambivalence, not even a mouse-squeak of it, [is] permitted. Celebrity moms love ... their kids unconditionally all the time; they love ... being mothers all the time."[2] The image of perfection, not only of lifestyle but of maintaining perfect *love* at all times, is impossible to live up to.

Nicole knows it, even when she can barely contain her rage at David for being so messy and leaving her to keep up appearances. Abby knows it, and she waves off the overtures of a fellow mother at the park, even though she could desperately use an adult to talk to. The supermom who is effortlessly superloving is the height of perfection that Abby cannot meet, and this causes her to feel isolated from other mothers, the very people who could understand her best.

This is her tragedy, and—though quietly tucked into an ordinary afternoon—it is not small.

I wasn't quite prepared for my first readers' reaction to these stories. I don't think any writer is, really, but early workshop discussions surprised me.

If you're one of the many sane and happy people who have never participated in a writer's workshop, here's how it works. The hopeful writer brings a new story to a group of other writers, and they read it. Then they gather around a conference room table and say—out loud, in brutal detail—everything they liked and didn't like about the piece. Suggestions fly for fixing problems with the setting or holes in the plot, and people pick apart the characters' psyches like so many armchair psychiatrists.

If you're lucky, your fellow writers are gentle, kind, and insightful, and their advice gives you new ways to think about your writing and a road map toward a finished product. I was blessed with, for the most part, truly excellent readers.

Still, each round of discussion brought up questions about how we read fiction, especially how men and women may read differently. My readers were often divided, and many were uncomfortable. Regarding "Recognition," one (childless, male) instructor said, "I'm not certain that these ideas about the parent-child relationship are an important enough revelation to build a story around."

This seems to me pretty clear evidence that men and women read texts differently and have some different priorities when it comes to deciding what makes a good story—or one worth telling at all. And if that's the case, to what extent should stories of women's experiences follow the traditional, "masculine" advice given to writers?

In the traditional structure of fiction, the protagonist is a person whose choices and actions give rise to the drama of the story, not someone who is tossed about by external events. Think of Huck Finn on his adventures and making his big choice at the end to free Jim, even though it's illegal. Think of all those tough Hemingway guys in their bullfights and battles. Author John Gardner expresses this view in *The Art of Fiction: Notes on Craft for Young Writers* when he says, "No fiction can have real interest if the central character is not an agent struggling for his or her own goals but a victim, subject to the will of others."[3] He goes on to describe a successful climax as one in which "we must be shown dramatically why each character believes what he does and why each cannot sympathize with the values of his antagonist."[3]

This assumes a lot about what kind of main characters are worthy of being written about. For one thing, it suggests that the central character always has agency — always has the power to change things. It also assumes that there's always an antagonist around to get in the way and create juicy conflicts. But what happens when all the drama is taking place inside your own body — and you don't have any control over it?

I would argue (and did, frequently) that this prescription for writing stories is limiting because it is a masculine construct that highlights the hero's journey and traditional man vs. man conflicts that have made up most of literature as we know it. Plenty of feminist scholars have criticized this masculine story construction, including Nancy K. Miller, who states that while "the plots of male fiction chart the daydreams of an ego that would be invulnerable ... the heroine's posture might well be a variant of Murphy's Law: If anything can go wrong, it will."[4] Miller takes issue with critics who dismiss women's stories as implausible because female protagonists lack clear motives and argues that the motives are unclear only to men, who are limited by the traditional view of a hero.

This rang true to me as I absorbed what readers had to say about these stories. For example, one of the difficult aspects of "September Air" for some readers — typically the ones without a uterus or children of their own—was their impatience with the pace of the beginning. Generally, the childless reader's criticism of the story is that "nothing happens" for the first nine pages, and when Abby finally "snaps" at the end, there is not a clear cause for it.

But for women and mothers the world 'round, the details of a daily routine aren't just exposition: they *are* the story. Abby's anger is not caused by any particular event; rather, it's the cumulative effect of daily frustrations and exhaustion. One reader, in discussing the pace, suggested that I "didn't have to tell the story exactly as it happened." Instead, I could speed it up by glossing some things. But my purpose in pacing the opening so slowly, with such claustrophobic detail, was to wear on the reader in the same way that Abby is worn down by her routine. To me, then, the complaint that the opening doesn't have enough happening is a sign that I have achieved my goal of making the reader as uncomfortable with the routine as Abby is.

I don't want to speed up and gloss over the so-called "boring" parts of women's lives because for many women who become mothers, boredom and frustration are major antagonists. Society's penchant for action in the quest or battle format of stories, which we have accepted for so long as the benchmark of fine literature—that story with the neat little triangle of rising and falling action that John Gardner presses upon aspiring writers—needs to be challenged. We need to tell women's stories, especially those of pregnancy, birth, and motherhood, which men can by definition never experience. My experience revising "September Air" left me, like many feminist authors and critics before me, calling out for new forms and a women's language of storytelling that would not be seen as problematic but as right and natural for the story I wanted to tell. If the traditional form of the short story demands what feminist scholars see as a masculine protagonist, how is a story of the quintessentially female act of pregnancy and birth to be written?

Of the four stories included here, "The Second Time" strikes me as the most traditional in many ways. Its conflict is more external than in the other stories, pitting a wife's emotional desire to preserve her pregnancy against her husband's intellectual, practical desire to terminate it. Here the personalities and desires of the characters are clearly counterpointed, and the female protagonist operates with a greater sense of free will than in the other stories.

Unlike the others, this story *does* follow the advice John Gardner offers to aspiring writers in *On Becoming a Novelist*. In Gardner's definition of plot, a "central character wants something, goes after it despite opposition (perhaps including his own doubts), and so arrives at a win, loss, or draw,"[5] and here Emmie wants to have her second child, despite Michael's arguments for the abortion.

The end results in a loss for Emmie, and she is left to come to terms with the loss of the baby and the strain on her marriage. Gardner also maintains in *The Art of Fiction: Notes on Craft for Young Writers* that in "serious fiction, [the] highest kind of suspense involves the Sartrian anguish of choice; that is, our suspenseful concern is not just with what will happen but with the moral implications of action."[3] In "The Second Time," Emmie and Michael struggle with the issue of ending the pregnancy: Emmie is greatly troubled by the thought of ending her baby's life, whereas Michael is concerned about the quality of life their daughter Sophie will have if she grows up with a brother with Down syndrome.

It is interesting to me, given the hot-button political and moral questions raised by the abortion in this story, that workshop readers in general found this story more "readable" than the others. Readers' acceptance of this story may have far more to do with its form than its content. There are no doubt readers who are not comfortable with Emmie's abortion, but because Emmie's conflict and choice follow the traditional—that is, masculine—pattern Gardner discusses, the story is less controversial than the other stories in the collection: the story meets traditional expectations of storytelling.

But surely this is not the only acceptable way to write a story, especially the largely untold stories of pregnancy and birth. There must be room in the world and on our bookshelves for a wide range of ways to wrestle with our humanity and struggle with what it means to live the life in the body you've been given. If your story doesn't fit the form, you need a different form. But tell it you must.

So what does it mean to be a protagonist when the events in your story are beyond your control? Susan Maushart defines pregnancy as a "blurring of the boundaries of selfhood, of where 'I' leaves off and 'You' begins [that] is a primary biological fact of pregnancy" [1]—and the main thing that separates stories of motherhood from any other trope. Each of the women in these stories has to come to terms with what, exactly, she can and cannot control, starting with her body. Julia feels completely unready to give birth, Emmie can't control the health of her baby, and Nicole waits in suspense to find out whether her body has gone ahead and conceived without her permission. Their bodies and their experience of motherhood are always, inevitably, just beyond their control.

In the end, it's Abby—despite her desperate moment breaking through the window screen—who is most in control. She does not, after all, harm her children, and the cuts on her arms are accidental. "Everyone wants to throw the baby out the window at some point," my sister-in-law told me when my daughter was born. "The only difference is that sane people don't actually do it." When Abby feels herself losing control, she gets away from her baby as quickly as she can. I would argue that she acts heroically by seizing control of her urge to strike her child and fighting it down to protect the baby. In the inevitable conflict that bubbles up in the parent/child relationship, someone must get hurt: a child physically, or the parent emotionally. Abby chooses to inflict these wounds on herself. She makes a choice; however constricted her options are, she does act.

The mother hero doesn't have to slay dragons—though she may do that too. She may also travel no farther than the nearest park with a swing set and a bench. Her work is internal, and that's as it must be. Having experienced what feminist Hélène Cixous called "the not-me within me,"[6] how could it be any other way? There is no manual for where the self ends and the new life begins in those early days, and you may spend a lifetime figuring out who you are now that you have had this experience.

In "The Yellow Wallpaper"—the seminal story of a woman coming to terms with an utter lack of control over anything in her life—Charlotte Perkins Gilman describes the protagonist's husband as a man who "has no patience with faith ... and scoffs openly at any talk of things not to be felt and seen and put down in figures."[7]

But I have felt things that I haven't seen: a tiny fist knocking on the far side of my ribcage and the ripples of hiccups that weren't mine. These things may have happened in darkness, invisible to the world, but they did happen, as they do every day to women around the world. Is any such miracle minor? I think not.

So tell your story. Seek them out from other women, too, because honest stories about real women and their pregnant bodies need to be told. When we do, we will also teach readers to understand them as they are, not as the readers assume they should be.

Notes

1. Susan Maushart, The Mask of Motherhood: How Becoming a Mother Changes Everything and Why We Pretend It Doesn't (New York: New Press, 1999).

2. Susan Douglas and Meredith Michaels, The Mommy Myth: The Idealization of Motherhood and How It Has Undermined Women (New York: Free Press, 2004).

3. John Gardner, The Art of Fiction: Notes on Craft for Young Writers (New York: A. Knopf, 1983).

4. Nancy K. Miller, "Emphasis Added: Plots and Plausibilities in Women's Fiction," in The New Feminist Criticism: Essays on Women, Literature, and Theory, ed. Elaine Showalter (New York: Pantheon Books, 1985), 339–60.

5. John Gardner, On Becoming a Novelist (New York: Harper & Row, 1983).

6. Lisa Walsh, "Writing (into) the Symbolic: The Maternal Metaphor in Hélène Cixous," in Language and Liberation: Feminism, Philosophy, and Language, eds. Christina Hendricks and Kelly Oliver (Albany: State University of New York Press, 1999), 347–66.

7. Charlotte Perkins Gilman, "The Yellow Wallpaper," in The Norton Anthology of Short Fiction, 6th ed., ed. R. V. Cassill and Richard Bausch (New York: Norton, 2000), 675–87.

Acknowledgements

Over the years that I wrote these stories, I was teaching—and growing babies—full time and working on my master's degree a semester at a time. None of that would have been possible without the support of many people along the way.

I'm grateful for the staff in the English department at UMass Boston. In particular, I'm thankful for the workshops of Joyce Peseroff and John Fulton and to my thesis readers, Askold Melnyczuk and Pamela Annas. I would never have been able to focus so exclusively on this work without a high-quality creative writing program at a public university that welcomes students of all stripes.

Thanks also to my friend Bud Jennings, teaching mentor and editor extraordinaire, who was an enthusiastic reader of late drafts.

I am also deeply appreciative to Melanie Nelson of Annorlunda Books for believing in my work, and to Francesca Forrest for her careful work in readying this collection for publication.

Finally, none of this would exist without my husband Kirk, who let me close the library door as often as I needed to. No one could ask for a better, more equal partner in life.

About the Author

Elizabeth Trach is a writer and editor living in Newburyport, Massachusetts. She earned her M.A. in Creative Writing at the University of Massachusetts, Boston, and her poetry has previously been published in The Worcester Journal. When not busy writing, she also sings in a band, grows almost all her own food, and occasionally even cooks it.

You can catch up on all of her adventures in extreme gardening at PortPotager.blogspot.com or read more of her work at TheBlogwright.com.

About the Publisher

Annorlunda Books is a small press that publishes books to inform, entertain, and make you think. We publish short writing (novella length or shorter), fiction or non-fiction. Our publication criteria are simple: if we like it and it taught us something new or made us think, we'll publish it.

Find more information about us and our books online at annorlundaenterprises.com/books/, on Facebook at facebook.com/annorlundabooks/, or on Twitter at @AnnorlundaInc.

To stay up to date on all of our releases, subscribe to our mailing list at annorlundaenterprises.com/mailing-list/

Other Titles from Annorlunda Books

Original Short eBooks and Collections

The Lilies of Dawn, by Vanessa Fogg, is a fantasy novelette about love, duty, family, and one young woman's coming of age.

The Burning, by J.P. Seewald, is a novella set in the coal country of Pennsylvania, about a family struggling to cope as a slow-moving catastrophe threatens everything they have..

Unspotted, by Justin Fox, is the story of the Cape Mountain Leopard, the scientist dedicated to saving these rare and elusive big cats, and the author's own journey to try to see one.

Caresaway, by DJ Cockburn, is a near future "inside your head" thriller about a scientist who discovers a cure for depression, but finds that it comes at a terrible cost.

Water into Wine, by Joyce Chng, is a novella set in a space-traveling future. The protagonist inherits a vineyard on a distant planet, and moves there to build a life, but an interstellar war intervenes and threatens everything.

Okay, So Look, by Micah Edwards, is a humorous, accurate and thought-provoking, retelling of The Book of Genesis.

Don't Call It Bollywood, by Margaret E. Redlich, is an introduction to the world of Hindi film, in which film history and analysis are interwoven with the author's personal stories of coming to love the art form.

Navigating the Path to Industry, by M.R. Nelson, is a hiring manager's advice on how to run a successful non-academic job search.

Academaze, by Sydney Phlox, is a collection of essays and cartoons about the tenure track and beyond at a research university.

Taster Flights

Hemmed In is a collection of classic short stories about women's lives.

Love and Other Happy Endings is a collection of classic short love stories that all end on a high note.

Missed Chances is another collection of classic stories about love. In each of its five stories, there is a hint of "the one that got away."

Small and Spooky is a collection of classic ghost stories that feature a child. These stories are spooky with a hint of sweet.

www.ingramcontent.com/pod-product-compliance
Lightning Source LLC
Chambersburg PA
CBHW032038180726
48284CB00008B/2649